Amelia Earhart

Young Aviator

Illustrated by Meryl Henderson

Amelia Earhart

Young Aviator

by Beatrice Gormley

ALADDIN PAPERBACKS

New York London Toronto Sydney

Dedicated to Shannon Gormley

First Aladdin Paperbacks edition February 2000

Text copyright © 2000 by Beatrice Gormley
Illustrations copyright © 2000 by Meryl Henderson

Aladdin Paperbacks
An imprint of Simon & Schuster Children's Publishing Division
1230 Avenue of the Americas
New York, NY 10020

20

Library of Congress Cataloging-in-Publication Data
Beatrice, Gormley.
Amelia Earhart: young aviator / by Beatrice Gormley ;
illustrated by Meryl Henderson.
1st Aladdin Paperbacks ed.
p.   cm.—(Childhood of Famous Americans)
ISBN-13: 978-0-689-83188-1
ISBN-10: 0-689-83188-9
1. Earhart, Amelia, 1897-1937—Juvenile literature. 2. Earhart, Amelia,
1897-1937—Childhood and youth—Juvenile literature. 3. Women air
pilots—United States—Biography—Juvenile literature.
I. Henderson, Meryl, illus. II. Title
Tl540.E3 G67   2000
[b]   99-59321
CIP AC
0312 OFF

Illustrations

Contents

Amelia Earhart

Young Aviator

Up in the Sky

One morning in the late spring of 1904, a girl with long blond braids leaned out the window of a train in the Kansas City railroad station.

"All aboard!" shouted the conductor from the platform. The last passengers hurried to climb into the cars. Porters in uniforms boosted the last trunks into the baggage car.

"We're already aboard," called seven-year-old Millie Earhart. The yellow bows on the ends of her braids brushed the side of the railroad car. "We're going to the World's Fair in St. Louis!"

Millie often rode the train from Kansas City, where the Earharts lived, to Grandma's house in Atchison. But that was just a short trip of an hour and a half. Today's trip was special.

The train ride to St. Louis would take all day, and they would stay there for a week. On their trips from Kansas City to Atchison, the Earharts always sat on hard wooden seats. But the seats in their Pullman car on this train were as soft and comfortable as the armchairs in the library at Grandma's house.

Millie (Amelia) sat next to her father, Edwin Earhart. In the two facing seats sat her mother, Amy Earhart, a pretty, slender woman, and Millie's younger sister, Pidge (Muriel). Like Millie, Pidge had big bows—green ones—on her braids. The girls both wore ruffled dresses of dotted swiss, long black stockings, and high-button shoes.

Unpinning her hat with the wide upturned brim, Mrs. Earhart handed it to her husband.

"Thank you, Edwin." Her delicate-featured face was beaming.

Smiling back with a little bow, Mr. Earhart put her hat and his own jaunty straw boater in the overhead rack. His wife pulled off her gloves, patted her upswept shiny brown hair, and settled the long skirts of her traveling dress.

"Meet me in St. Louie, Amy," Mr. Earhart sang to his wife. He was handsome, his dark straight hair slicked down with pomade. He wore a light summer suit and a silver watch chain across his vest.

"Dad," said Pidge seriously, "*Amy* doesn't rhyme with *Louie*." Silly four-and-a-half-year-old Pidge! Millie grinned at her father, and he winked back. Dad knew that Millie knew he was having fun with a popular song, "Meet Me in St. Louis, Louis."

Just for a moment, Millie wondered why Grandma didn't think this trip was a good idea. The day before yesterday, Mother had arrived in Atchison to pick up Millie for the summer. She had told Grandma and Grandpa about the coming trip to St. Louis. Millie remembered Grandpa saying to Mother, "I suppose Edwin has bought tickets for a *Pullman* car." Grandma had put in, with a disapproving sniff, "As if this jaunt to the fair weren't extravagance enough!"

Mother had flushed and answered them, "The trip will take all day. Edwin wants us to be comfortable." Then the grown-ups noticed Millie, and they had stopped talking.

Now the train pulled out of the cavernous Kansas City station and into the bright light of the May morning. The two girls knelt on their seats to look out the window. As the wheels clicked faster and faster, the train slid past the drab narrow houses where poor people lived. Their backyards were barely big enough for a clothesline, where their long underwear hung out for everyone to see.

For a split second—but it seemed longer—

Millie stared into the solemn face of a girl her age, sitting on the rickety steps of one of the houses. Then she turned away to see her mother watching her. "Mother," said Millie, "I wish everyone could go to the World's Fair."

"So do I, dear," said Mrs. Earhart.

The train left the city behind, and now farmland spread out as far as they could see. Rows of corn, already tall, flicked past like the riffled pages of a book. "Look, Pidge," said Millie, "look at the telegraph poles by the tracks, how fast they're going by." Her little sister obediently blinked at the line of poles flashing past the train window. "Now look at that barn and silo across the field, how slow *they're* going. See? You can make the train seem to go fast or slow, just by looking here or there."

The train would pull them all the way across the state of Missouri. Mother had showed Millie and Pidge on a map. "When we cross the Missouri River *here*," Mother had said, tapping the squiggly line with a shapely fingernail, "we'll be halfway to St. Louis. When we cross it again, we'll be almost there."

Soon the girls were tired of looking out the window, and Millie got Dad to tell one of his made-up stories about the Wild West. "Just then another shot rang out." Mr. Earhart clutched his chest, slumping in his seat. "'They've got me, Mac,' I groaned."

Then Mother read aloud from *Black Beauty*, a story about a horse. They had gotten to the part in which a drunken man whipped Black Beauty to make him gallop, although the horseshoe had fallen off one hoof. As the girls listened, tears welled up in Pidge's eyes. But Millie's eyes flashed. "I would make that man stop whipping his horse," she said.

"I'll bet you would, too," said Dad, giving her shoulders a squeeze.

The train clickety-clacked across the

Missouri River on high trestles, and it was time for lunch in the dining car. This was as fancy as dinners at Grandma's, with a white linen tablecloth, flowers in a vase, and silver forks and knives. The Earharts ate chicken fricassee, new peas, and lemon layer cake.

Back in the Pullman car after lunch, Pidge fell asleep with her head in Mother's lap. Millie and Dad and Mother played quiet games of old maid.

Later, Dad read to them from a newspaper about the World's Fair. The first day, there would be a grand procession. There would be elephant rides and a Ferris wheel. There would be people from the other side of the world: from Africa, Japan, the Philippine Islands. There would be exhibits of amazing inventions: a railroad car with *electric* lights, a wireless telegraph tower, flying machines.

Millie sat up straight. "*Flying* machines? Can we fly in them?"

Mr. and Mrs. Earhart laughed. Mother

said, "I don't know that *anyone* can fly in them—at least, fly and land in one piece. Last year, the government paid Mr. Langley at the Smithsonian fifty thousand dollars to build a flying machine. When he tried it out —" She paused to laugh again.

"When he tried it out, this is what happened," continued Dad. He showed the girls by doing a nosedive with his hand. "Splat! At least Mr. Langley had the good sense to launch his contraption over the Potomac River."

The next morning, the Earharts hurried to the fair grounds to see the procession. As they watched from grandstand seats, there was a stir of excitement in the crowd. "Roosevelt's Rough Riders!" people around them exclaimed. A unit of cavalry soldiers trotted into view. Millie couldn't take her eyes off the riders, with their dashing cowboy hats and blue bandannas. She admired the easy way they handled their prancing horses.

After the procession, the Earharts set out to explore the fair grounds. All around them fountains sparkled in the sunlight, and marble statues gleamed among the flower beds. Crowds of people dressed in their summer best strolled along the paths.

Millie's eyes followed a tall column in the middle of the plaza to its top, where a statue perched on top of a globe. Then her gaze shifted to a section beyond the plaza and a little train of open cars swooping along a high track. "Oh! Look at that!"

"That's a roller coaster, one of the rides in the Midway," said Mr. Earhart.

"Dad!" Millie swung his hand, looking up with shining eyes. "Let's ride on it."

Mr. Earhart put on a mock-serious look. Of course he was going to say yes; he wanted to ride on the roller coaster, too. And he would never be so mean as to go on the roller coaster and leave Millie behind.

But before Mr. Earhart could answer, Mrs.

Earhart spoke up. "Absolutely not, Millie. I'm sure there are no other girls on the roller coaster."

"But, Mother!" protested Millie. "When you were a girl and wanted to climb Pike's Peak, what if Grandpa said, 'Absolutely not'? What if he'd told you, 'Girls have never done it before'?"

"Climbing Pike's Peak wasn't dangerous," said Mrs. Earhart. "And I was twenty-one." Mother was usually reasonable, but she had made up her mind.

"Let's ride on the Ferris wheel instead," said Mr. Earhart, squeezing Millie's hand. "We'll all ride." He nodded toward an enormous wheel, looming above the trees in the distance.

"Hooray!" shouted Millie. "Come on, Pidge!" She seized her sister's hand.

"Hooray, we're going on the Ferris wheel!" squealed Pidge. The girls skipped ahead of their parents, down the broad path to the Midway.

But in the shadow of the Ferris wheel, Pidge stopped and stared up with big round eyes. Without a word she let go of Millie's hand, ran to her mother, and buried her face in her skirts. Mrs. Earhart gazed wistfully up at the chattering, laughing passengers on the Ferris wheel, and she stroked Pidge's hair. "I'll wait for you," she told her husband. "Pidge will keep me company, won't you, dear?"

"Pidge, don't you want to go?" urged Millie. "It'll be such fun!" Often she could talk her sister into trying new things, but Mother was shaking her head no. So with a wave, Millie skipped alongside Dad to the ticket booth and climbed into the Ferris wheel seat. The wheel turned, the car rose into the air. Millie caught her breath with delight.

Then the wheel paused, and their car lurched and swung back and forth. Millie laughed. "We're like ants on a wagon wheel, aren't we, Dad?" Glancing down at Mother and Pidge, she saw her sister clap her hand over her mouth, as if she expected Millie to plummet to the ground before her eyes. "Don't worry, Pidge!"

The cars were all full now, and the wheel turned smoothly. Higher Millie rose, and higher. Higher than the treetops, higher than the Louisiana Monument. Millie looked down on the fairgrounds, on the city of St. Louis, and out to the horizon. Puffy clouds sat on the edge of the plain, and it seemed to Millie that she was higher than those clouds. "Dad," she said softly. "We're up in the sky."

Millie hated to have that ride end. But as soon as she was back on the ground, the roller coaster caught her eye again. Standing almost underneath the track, she watched the cars racketing uphill, downhill, around curves. The passengers shrieked and moaned, and one lady's hat flew off, but none of the people actually fell out of the roller coaster.

"Mother—" Millie started to point this out.

But Mr. Earhart changed the subject before Millie could even bring it up. "Who wants to eat ice cream without a dish?" he asked, beckoning them toward a stand. "See that boy eating ice cream from a baked cone? What a good idea!"

Millie loved ice cream, and this new way of eating it made it taste twice as good. But as she licked her peach ice cream from the crisp cone, an idea came to her. The idea was even more delicious than the sweet, soft, creamy dessert on her tongue.

When she got home, she would build her own roller coaster.

At the end of their week at the World's Fair, Mr. Earhart went back to his office in Kansas City. Mother and Millie and Pidge went to Atchison for a visit. The first morning at Grandma's house, Millie gulped down her waffle and her glass of milk. Uncle Carl, one of Mother's brothers, winked at Millie across the breakfast table. "What big plans do the Katzenjammer Kids have today?"

Millie only grinned at him for an answer. He meant that she and Pidge were like the two boys in the Katzenjammer Kids comic strip, always up to some mischief. Millie wouldn't mind telling Uncle Carl her plans, but it was better not to talk in front of Grandma and Grandpa and Mother. "May we be excused from the table, Grandma? Come on, Pidge."

The girls ran out the back door and down the back porch steps into the yard. The June day was hot already, but a breeze from the river rustled the leaves on the big shade trees. Sniffing the scent of sun-warmed grass, Millie stared up at the roof of the toolshed. Yes. The toolshed would be just about the right height. Now, if that lumber was still in the barn . . .

In a dim corner of the barn, Millie found

long pieces of two-by-fours. The two-by-fours were heavy and awkward, but Millie was strong. With Pidge's help, she dragged the lengths of wood from the barn, then went back for a ladder.

As they were propping the first piece of lumber against the toolshed roof, a friend from school, Balie Waggener, strolled into the backyard. "A roller coaster?" Balie's eyes lit up when Millie explained her plan. "No fooling! Wait, I'll be right back." He ran home to get his tool chest.

During the morning more boys and girls came by, and some of them stayed to help. They sawed and hammered ties for the track. One end of the track they nailed to the ridgepole of the shed. For the roller coaster car, they found a crate and fastened old roller skates to its bottom. The skate wheels were a bit rusty, but Millie oiled them.

"We should grease the track, too," suggested Balie. They sent Pidge to the kitchen

to sneak a pail of lard from the icebox when the cook's back was turned.

After the boards were well greased, Millie scrambled back up to the roof of the shed. Balie and another boy pushed the crate from below while Millie pulled it up to the top of the track. "Now!" breathed Millie.

It took a few minutes, though, to get the roller coaster car in position. Just as Millie started to climb into the car, it rolled down the track by itself. They had to haul it up again. But Millie wasn't discouraged. "Did you see how it flew?" she exclaimed.

Finally the car was poised on the ridge-pole, with several hands steadying it from the ladder. Millie eased herself into the car. "Now—let go!"

In one glorious instant, Millie swooped down the track. She had just time to shout, "Whoo!" before the wheels hit the grass. The car and Millie flipped end over end.

Millie lay on the grass with the breath

knocked out of her, squinting up at Pidge's and Balie's anxious faces, backlighted by the sun. "Oh, Millie! Should I tell Mother?"

"Are you all right, Millie?"

Struggling to draw in a breath, Millie began to laugh. "Wasn't that grand?"

"Millie!" called a man's voice. Uncle Carl pounded down the steps of the back porch and across the lawn. But as soon as he saw Millie laughing, he started to laugh, too. "You crazy kids! You know," he went on thoughtfully, "if you made the track longer, it wouldn't be so steep."

Uncle Carl also had some good advice about using a sawhorse to prop up the middle of the longer track. "Like a trestle in the railroad bridge, you know?"

After lunch they finished rebuilding the track, and then Balie took a turn. "Whoo!" he shouted, just as Amelia had. But this time the car rolled on across the lawn without somersaulting.

As the shadows of the trees crept across the lawn, the children rode their roller coaster over and over. Two or three times, they decided they were too tired for one more ride. But then the cousins next door appeared, or friends from down the street came by. After the newcomers had taken turns, the others were eager to fly down the track again.

At supper, Grandma smiled down the table and asked, "What were you playing today, dears?" Mother added, "Yes, you sounded as if you were having such fun."

Millie exchanged glances with Pidge and Uncle Carl. If she told the truth, that would be the end of their roller coaster. . . . Well, she *had* to tell the truth.

The next morning was just as hot and sunny as the day before, but this was a sad day. Instead of the exciting ring of hammers on nails, the air was torn with the screech of nails pulling out of wood. Grandma had told Charlie, the handyman, to tear down the roller coaster. Millie and Pidge had to help carry the lumber back into the barn.

Still, thought Millie, they had had some glorious rides!

Millie Rides

During the school year, Millie stayed with Grandma and Grandpa Otis in Atchison, in their big house on North Terrace, overlooking the bluffs of the Missouri River. Millie had come to live with Grandma when she was only three, because Grandma was lonely. Millie could understand why someone would be lonely, living with Grandpa.

Judge Otis, a lean man with a trim gray beard and heavy eyebrows, was a very important person in Atchison. But he was no fun—he never wanted to do anything except work.

31

Millie was told she mustn't bother him in his study.

Grandma, round and dumpy with her gray hair coiled on top of her head, was "Amelia," too. Millie had been named after her. Grandma was not exactly *fun*, but she could be good company. She would play dominoes with Millie, or tell stories about the old days.

One November evening they were settled by the fire, Grandma in her rocker with her knitting and Millie on the hearthrug with a book. "My, how Atchison has changed since I came East to Kansas as a young bride," said Grandma. "I was a Harres of Philadelphia, you know."

Millie put a finger in her book to mark her place. "Were there still Indians in Atchison then?"

"Oh yes, indeed," said Grandma. "I was afraid to go shopping downtown. The Indians came right up to me and felt the cloth of my dress! They peeked into my shopping basket."

Millie wouldn't have been scared of the Indians, she was sure of that. "And were there buffalo then, real buffalo?"

"Yes, great herds. The railroads had to shoot them so the locomotives could get through. There used to be piles of buffalo bones beside the railroad tracks." Grandma paused in her knitting and gazed into the fire with a faraway look. "After the war"—Millie knew she meant the Civil War—"Atchison was the place where pioneer wagon trains started for California or Oregon."

Sighing, Millie rolled over on the hearthrug. She had missed the time of adventure, the pioneer days. It was too bad!

Still, she was happy to live in Atchison, even now. When she went to Kansas City, where her mother and father and sister lived, she had to share a room with Pidge. The Earharts' house in Kansas City was small, with a tiny porch and narrow yard.

At Grandma's, Millie played on broad

lawns and wandered through the flower gardens and orchard and grape arbor. There was a wide veranda across the front of the handsome white house. On the second floor Millie slept in her own spacious bedroom, with windows that looked out into the sky and down to the river. This same room had once belonged to her great-grandmother, Maria Harres. Years ago Great-grandma had saved Mother's life, when she was choking to death from diphtheria.

Another thing Millie liked about Grandma's: it was right next door to the big brick house where the Challiss cousins lived. The two oldest Challiss girls, Lucy ("Toot") and Kathryn ("Katch"), were always there to play with. And close by was the school Millie walked to every morning. There were more friends at school, like Ginger Park and Balie Waggener.

Yes, Grandma's house was almost perfect, except for one thing. "Grandma?" Millie

34

spoke up in her most reasonable voice. "Don't you think it's a shame to have a barn with perfectly good horse stalls going to waste?" The Otises hated to have anything go to waste.

"Our barn? Why, we don't need horses, dear. We live in town, and the tradesmen deliver meat and groceries and so on. When we need a carriage, we hire it from the livery stable, or use your Uncle Challiss's."

"But if we had a horse, I could learn to ride." Millie gave Grandma her brightest smile.

"No, dear. It's too dangerous."

"But you used to let Mother ride, when she was a girl. She had her own Indian pony."

Resting her knitting in her lap, Grandma looked at Millie over her glasses. "Amelia. You are not to tease."

Millie was silent. Would it do any good to tell Grandma about Circus, a horse Mother rode in the days when she was still Amy Otis?

Amy had discovered that Circus really was a horse from the circus. He knew a circus trick: He would dance on his hind legs if you twitched the reins just the right way. Amy had never let Circus perform in front of her mother, though. And Millie had a feeling that probably Mother still didn't want Grandma to know about it.

Rolling over on the hearthrug again, Millie turned back to her book, *Black Beauty*. One of the horses was explaining what it was like to wear a checkrein:

"Fancy now yourself, if you tossed your head up high and were obliged to hold it there, and that for hours together, not able to move it at all, except with a jerk still higher, your neck aching till you did not know how to bear it. Besides that, to have two bits instead of one; and mine was a sharp one, it hurt my tongue and my jaw, and the blood from my tongue colored the froth that kept flying from my lips, as I chafed and fretted at the bits and rein . . . Besides the soreness in my mouth and the pain in my neck, it always made my windpipe feel bad . . ."

Millie had already read *Black Beauty* many times, and before that Mother had read it aloud to her and Pidge. But she still got angry all over again when she read this part. It made her want to jump into the story and help the poor horse.

Early the next morning, Millie came down to the kitchen to see what was for breakfast. "Good morning, Mary," she said to the cook, who was turning sausage patties. Then she noticed the coal man's wagon outside, by the cellar door.

Look at the coal man's horse! Foam dropped from his mouth as he jerked his head up. He tried to jerk it down, but he was stopped by the cruel checkrein. Just as Millie had read in *Black Beauty*!

The coal man was out of sight. Grabbing a

warm biscuit from a rack on the counter, Millie slipped out the kitchen door. "Don't worry, old fellow," Millie told the horse, patting his neck. She put one foot on the shaft of the wagon and clambered up onto his back.

The leather strap of the checkrein was thick and stiff, but Millie pried it out of the buckle and rebuckled it in the lowest notch. Now the horse snorted and tossed his head all the way up and all the way down, making his forelock fly. "Doesn't that feel better?" whispered Millie. Climbing down, she fed him the biscuit and then scooted back into the house.

Nobody had seen what Millie did. But the coal man was angry when he found the checkrein lowered. He complained to Mary, the cook, and she remembered Millie going outside for a few minutes. Mary told Grandpa, and Grandpa took Millie aside after breakfast.

"The horse is the coal man's property,

Amelia," said Grandpa. He rocked back and forth on his black square-toed shoes, making them creak. "As a matter of law, you had no right to meddle with it."

"Yes, Grandpa," said Millie. She gave Judge Otis a straight look from her gray eyes. "But . . . the coal man had no right to be so mean to his horse, either."

It was satisfying to help that poor horse, but Millie hadn't given up her idea of riding. She could imagine so well her dream horse, a palomino of Arabian blood. She would name him Saladin, after the noble enemy of King Richard the Lion-Hearted.

On the way home from school one day, Millie saw her chance to ride. She was walking past the butcher's house—the same butcher who delivered Grandma's order of roasts and chops every week—when she noticed three girls in the stable yard. One of them was sitting on the back of a horse.

"Hello," called Millie. "I wish I had a horse to ride, like you."

"He's only one of Pa's delivery wagon horses," said the girl shyly. "We're allowed to ride them when business is slow." She patted the gray workhorse's neck. "Do you want a turn?"

Millie didn't need a second invitation. She skipped into the stable yard and climbed the fence to mount the horse. "Easy, Saladin," she said, as if he were a spirited steed that needed to be soothed.

"His name is Pokey," said the youngest girl helpfully.

Pokey was a better name, Millie had to admit, for this swaybacked, stodgy animal. But still, there she was on the back of a real horse! Up here, she felt so big and powerful, it made her laugh out loud. She rode the horse around the stable yard, then around the block. She was almost as happy as if she were on the prancing Arabian mount of her imagination.

After that, Millie would stop by the butcher's on the way home from school. Sometimes she rode the other delivery horse, a sorrel of a lovely orange-brown color. He had a little more spirit than Pokey, and once or twice he tried to buck her off. *That* was fun.

Late one afternoon, Millie came home whistling from a nice ride at the butcher's house. This arrangement was just perfect. Millie could ride whenever she wanted to. At the same time, Grandma didn't get upset, because she didn't know about it.

Running up to the picket fence, Millie vaulted it smoothly, still whistling. But just short of the steps to the veranda, Millie paused. Grandma was standing in the front doorway, and a frown creased her forehead.

"*Amelia.* I'm very disappointed in you. You must stop this unladylike behavior."

Millie's heart sank. Grandma must have found out about her secret riding! Who had told her—the butcher? Surely not the girls.

"Think how it looks, Millie, when your skirt flies up and your stockings show."

"I'm sorry, Grandma," said Millie, smoothing the skirt of her dress over her black stockings. She was even more puzzled. How did Grandma know how it looked? She had been here in the house while Millie was riding the butcher's horse.

"Ladylike girls do not jump fences," Grandma went on. "It isn't fitting for any girls, but especially not for an Otis girl. We have a position to uphold in Atchison, you know."

Millie nodded meekly, but inside she was smiling with relief. "Jump fences!" Grandma had only been scolding her for jumping over the fence. Millie could give *that* up—for a while, anyway.

For several days, Millie made a show of opening the front gate and walking through it like a little lady. After a week or so, she circled around the yard to a place where she could vault the fence out of Grandma's sight. Meanwhile—she paid regular visits to the butcher's horses.

Every year, when school was out for the summer, Millie left Grandma's house in Atchison and went to stay with her mother and father and Pidge in Kansas City, fifty miles away. She missed her school friends and her cousins and her big bedroom all to herself, but it was great fun to be home with her father and sister and mother. They didn't have to be so proper at meals. And Mother was much more sensible than Grandma was—for instance, about creepy-crawly creatures.

Millie and Pidge made a game of finding interesting creatures and looking up their names in Millie's book *Insect Life*. They found a pale green luna moth and several katydids and a praying mantis. Mrs. Earhart gave them a box with a screen top for their collection, and let them keep it on the porch. The girls called their collection "the museum." Uncle Carl called it "the bug party."

Amy Earhart, still slender and pretty, loved nice clothes for herself. She liked Millie and Pidge to wear pretty dresses, too. But she didn't scold them, as Grandma would have, for hanging upside down from the overhead bar of the lawn swing. Instead, she surprised them one day with special playsuits.

"They're called 'gymnasium suits,'" said Mrs. Earhart, holding up one of the navy blue flannel outfits with bloomer legs and white sailor collars. "Your aunt Margaret is right; girls ought to be able to play without worrying about modesty."

Pulling on their gymnasium suits, Millie and Pidge ran outside. Millie stretched her legs farther with each step. So this was the way boys felt all the time, this free!

"What does Mother mean, 'modesty'?" panted Pidge as she climbed up on the lawn swing after Millie.

"She means, not showing your underdrawers when you . . ." Hooking her long legs over the bar, Millie swung upside down. From her new position, she noticed two faces above the back fence. Those girls who always wore frilly, ruffled dresses were watching.

"They'll tell everyone we're odd," whispered Pidge.

Millie, still upside down, called to the neighbor girls in her loudest, most cheerful voice, "You should try this. It's fun!"

The very best thing about summers in Kansas City, Millie thought, was spending time with her father. Amy Earhart and Pidge often came to Atchison to visit Grandma and Grandpa, but Edwin Earhart hardly ever came with them. And when he did come to Atchison, he wasn't as much fun as he was at home.

But in Kansas City, it was different. Edwin Earhart was a lawyer, like Grandpa, but he wasn't like Alfred Otis in any other way. Dad spent the weekends playing games with Millie and Pidge.

Mr. Earhart told the girls wild adventure stories, making them up as he went along. In the evenings after dinner, he loved to tinker. He would cover the kitchen table with newspapers and bring out his tools and whatever gadget he was working on. Millie and Pidge sat at the table with their chins propped on their hands, watching him work.

When Mr. Earhart was away on business, he wrote the girls letters, sticking in hard words that they had to look up in the dictionary. "Dear parallelepipedon," began one of his letters to Millie.

"Dear Dad," Millie wrote back. "Kindly do not call me a parallelepipedon, because I have *more* than six sides. Yesterday Pidge and I had worm races. I don't know who won, it was hard to make the worms stay on the track."

Adventures

Even in the summer, if Mr. Earhart was away on business, Mrs. Earhart and Millie and Pidge often rode the train to Atchison to visit Grandma. On one of those visits, Millie decided to teach her cousin Katch to ride a bicycle. She had already taught Pidge, and Ginger Park's little sister, Ann, and it would be too bad for Katch to be left out. She could learn on Pidge's bicycle, which was about the right size.

"Hang on, Katch!" Millie ran alongside while Katch, perched on the seat, clutched the handlebars. Millie kept one hand on the back of the seat to steady the bicycle and give it a push. "Pedal faster! It'll stay up better, the faster you go. That's it!" Katch leaned forward and pedaled harder, and Toot and Pidge cheered from the side of the road.

It was a shame, in Millie's opinion, that her cousins weren't allowed to wear gymnasium suits instead of dresses to play in. Everything was easier and freer in pants: walking on stilts, hanging upside down, riding a bicycle.

Still, it was wonderful to see Katch's expression, her blue-green eyes wide and her mouth open in a breathless smile as she wobbled along Second Street. Katch was doing something she'd never done before—ride a bicycle. In a way, thought Millie, helping Katch was as good as learning to do something new herself. "Now turn, Katch!" The younger girl steered the bicycle in a shaky U-turn.

By the time Katch was getting the hang of it, the sky had darkened, and fat drops of rain began to splash in the dust. Millie and Toot led the younger girls in a dash across the yards to the Otises' barn.

With the thunderstorm outside, it was darker than usual in the barn. But the girls all knew exactly where they were going—to the old carriage, to play "Bogie." They clambered over the cracked leather seats, sneezing at the dust. Pidge and Katch settled in back. Millie and Toot, with the natural rights of older sisters, sat in front.

Picking up the reins, Millie clucked to the imaginary team of horses. She intoned in her "story" voice, "They had been traveling all day, yet they seemed no closer than ever to their destination, Pearyville."

Toot took up the game. "Isn't it about time we were getting into the next town?"

"*If* we're on the right road," said Millie in an ominous tone, "we ought to make it by nightfall."

"Let's see a map," Katch piped up from the

backseat. "This place doesn't look familiar to me." (Of course Katch wanted to get out the map. She had drawn their map of Bogie, and she was very proud of it.)

The driver halted the imaginary horses, and they all studied the map. They should have been nearing the woods and the Red Lion Inn, but they hadn't even passed Witches' Cove yet. Had they somehow taken the wrong turn after the Bridge of Skeletons?

"I don't remember these swamps at all," declared Toot. "And not a house in sight. Anything might happen."

"WHAT'S THAT OVER THERE?" Holding the reins with one hand, Millie pointed dramatically into the swamp that Toot had mentioned.

Playing Bogie, anything could happen.

On other days, when the weather was good, Millie's favorite place to play was the bluffs. Ginger Park, her best school friend, often came along. They never went all the way down to the banks, but it was exciting to be near the river. The Missouri was yellow with mud and swirling with dangerous-looking whirlpools. Here and there on the bluffs, there were caves in the yellow sandstone.

Sometimes Millie would stand still at the top of the bluffs, watching a hawk floating in slow circles. Once in a while, a hawk would fold its wings and plunge at heart-pounding speed toward its prey. It gave Millie a floating, soaring feeling, to see the bird so sure and bold in the empty air.

But Millie's own adventures, even imaginary ones, took place on the ground. "I've heard there's buried treasure down there!" Millie would call to Ginger and the others. She would lead the way down the bluffs through the brambles and scrub trees, over ledges.

Sometimes the girls wanted to be quiet, and then they would go inside to the Otises' library and stretch out on the floor with a book or magazine. When they were younger, their favorites were the Beatrix Potter stories: *Peter Rabbit*, about a young bunny who plunged recklessly into danger, or *The Tailor of Gloucester*, with the cat Simpkin who was finally ashamed of his selfishness.

Later, the girls lost themselves in the funny and sad and exciting novels by Charles Dickens and Sir Walter Scott and Alexander Dumas. In the magazines, there were sometimes thrilling real-life stories about adventurers like the Arctic explorer Robert Peary. Wonderful, wonderful stories—but why did the best adventures always happen to boys, even in books? Toot and Ginger agreed with Millie that it wasn't fair.

At school, too, the best games seemed to be reserved for boys—basketball, for instance. Watching the boys on the playground, running and leaping and shooting baskets, Millie decided there was no reason why she and the other girls shouldn't play.

She went straight to the captain of the basketball team, a senior boy, and got him to explain the rules. Then she taught Ginger and Toot. The girls began to play on a field across the street from the Otises', where there was an iron basketball hoop fastened to the side of the barn.

Millie had been going to the College Preparatory School, a small private school, ever since first grade. She did well in her studies, and she could have won the mathematics prize for the lower school, two years in a row. The headmistress, Sarah Walton, shook her head. "If only you had written down the steps by which you solved the problems, Millie . . ."

Millie was just as glad that Ginger had won the mathematics prize instead. "I don't especially care about the prize," she explained politely to Miss Walton. "I know that I understand how to get the answers, and so do you— so what's the difference who has the medal?"

* * *

In 1908, Millie's life began to change.

First, Mr. Earhart took a new job, in the claims office of the Rock Island Railroad Line. It was a good steady job, but it meant that he and Mrs. Earhart and Millie and Pidge would have to move from Kansas City to Des Moines, Iowa. That summer, the Earharts took the two-hundred-mile trip to Des Moines to look over the city.

While they were in Des Moines, they went to the Iowa State Fair. They had to see the new inventions, of course, because Edwin Earhart loved inventions so much. In fact, Millie realized now, it was something about an invention that had turned Grandma and Grandpa against him, years ago.

He had *gambled* (Grandma said that word to Aunt Margaret with such disgust) the property tax money on an invention of his. The money was lost, and Dad had to sell the valuable law books that Grandpa had given him. "Not a good provider," Aunt Margaret had agreed with Grandma.

Now, just outside the state fair's Hall of Inventions, Millie stopped to buy a funny-looking paper hat for a few pennies. Then she hurried to catch up with Dad and Mother and Pidge. They had paused in front of a contraption made of wood and canvas, with a seat in the middle.

"Look, Millie, it's one of those flying machines," said Mrs. Earhart, pointing to the sign. "They keep trying!"

"I heard that someone in upstate New York flew a whole mile the other day," said Mr. Earhart. He posed with one hand on his chest and the other stretched out, like an opera singer. "Come, Josephine, in my flying machine," he warbled.

Millie ran her eyes over the invention, a clumsy structure held together with struts and wires. Even if it did fly, it couldn't fly as well as a bird or a dragonfly. It wasn't graceful, like a horse or a ship, or fast, like a train. Nothing about it captured her imagination.

"Look, Pidge, I'm a very fashionable lady." Pulling her paper hat down over her forehead, Millie strolled past the flying machine with a silly mincing walk.

Pidge giggled. "It looks like you're wearing a peach basket!"

That December, when Millie was eleven, she knew this would be her last Christmas in Atchison. The Earharts had already sold the house in Kansas City. Pidge was living with Grandma, too, but she and Millie would stay only until their parents found a new home in Des Moines.

On Christmas Eve, Mr. and Mrs. Earhart arrived, their arms full of mysterious packages. Millie and Pidge went into a corner to whisper about what they might be. "I wrote Dad a letter asking for footballs," said Millie. "But what are those two big flat things?"

The next morning, when the family gathered in the parlor, Mr. Earhart grinned at the girls as they unwrapped the "big flat things."

"New sleds!" they chorused. Not poky girls' sleds, for sitting up and sliding feet first. No, two sleek low boys' sleds, with steel instead of wooden runners, for swooping downhill headfirst.

Grandma looked horrified, and Millie knew why. "Don't worry," Millie told her. "Pidge and I'll wear leggings when we sled, won't we?"

"Oh yes!" her sister chimed in. "And long coats." They didn't need to add, *So no one will see our underdrawers.*

A few weeks later, the sledding runs in the neighborhood were worn as slick as glass, so you could get up a good speed. Millie launched herself from the top of the steepest hill with a thwacking belly flop. "Whoo-ee!" Faster and faster she flew downhill, her eyes almost closed against the wind.

Then Millie's eyes popped wide open. On the street below, the junkman was driving his cart slowly across the sled track. "Watch out!" she yelled, but he didn't hear. She wrenched at the sled, but it wouldn't swerve on the icy run. There was nothing to do but plunge on down to the road—straight between the legs of the junkman's horse.

Later Millie told Grandma the story, thinking to make her feel happier that her granddaughters were riding boys' sleds. "You see, if I'd been sitting up on my old sled, I probably would've been killed," she explained cheerfully. Grandma gasped and pressed one hand to the base of her throat.

As it turned out, it took Mother and Dad a long time to find just the right house in Des Moines. In March the country got a new president, President William Taft, and Millie and Pidge were still at Grandma's. On April 6 the explorer Robert Peary reached the North

Pole. Millie pored over the newspaper stories: Peary had almost frozen to death, but he had driven his dogsled four hundred miles to plant the American flag at the top of the world.

That July, the Earharts took a vacation at Lake Okabena in Minnesota, as they had last year and the year before. Then the girls returned to Atchison. They missed Dad, but they had the fun of exchanging letters with him. In one of his letters to Pidge, Mr. Earhart pretended that she had filed a claim against the railroad because a mosquito had bitten her during her last train ride. "This case will probably have to be referred to the Chicago office," he wrote solemnly, "as it is so serious a case and I hardly feel like handling it."

At Grandma's, the best part of a summer day was the long twilight after dinner. The air on those evenings, filled with the humming and chirping of insects and tree frogs, was thick and hot. It wilted the grown-ups. They sat on the veranda fanning themselves, while

Millie and Pidge ran around the flower beds.

Toot and Katch, next door, would call from their house for Millie and Pidge to come over. Running to the fence between the yards, Millie boosted Pidge over, then climbed the fence herself into the Challisses' yard. The sunset faded as the four girls played until the Second Street light came on. That meant it was time for Millie and Pidge to go home.

That summer of 1909 was the last time that Millie's home *was* the big white house on the bluffs of the Missouri River.

A Happy, Lucky Family

Living in Des Moines, Millie missed her grand-mother and her cousins and friends in Atchison. But she kept up with Toot and Katch and Ginger and Ann through letters, and some-times they came to visit. Besides, it was fun to live with Mother and Dad and Pidge.

On weekends, when Mr. Earhart wasn't traveling on business, he would take the girls fishing in the Des Moines River. Their mother let them wear jeans, just as if they were boys. Their father gave them bamboo poles, and they wore straw hats to keep off the sun.

Part of the fun of fishing trips was Dad's stories about when he was growing up on the "wrong side of the tracks" in Atchison. "My father was a Lutheran preacher, you know," Dad explained one day as he rowed them out on the river. "He was very strict about keeping the Sabbath, and that meant no fishing on Sundays."

But one Sunday young Edwin sneaked out anyway and caught six plump catfish. His mother begged his father to let the children eat them. "The young ones are hungry, and there is no food in the house but cornmeal and turnips."

Edwin put in, "You know the fish always bite better when you are preaching, sir." His father had to smile. In the end, the whole family, including the Reverend Earhart, had feasted on panfried catfish that day.

In Atchison, Millie and Pidge were known as Judge Otis's granddaughters, but here in Des Moines they were known as the daughters of Chief Indian. Saturday afternoon games of "Indians" became a tradition in the Earharts' neighborhood. All the boys and girls would gather in time to meet their hero, Mr. Earhart, as he arrived home from the office on the streetcar. Playing the part of Chief Indian, he would lead an exciting chase around the house, yard, and barn.

Once, as Mr. Earhart poked his head into the hayloft and the children tried to close the sliding door on him, he had his nose severely banged. But there were no hard feelings. After the game, friends and "enemies" all drank lemonade together on the porch.

In the evenings, when the Earharts were sitting around the dinner table, they would have lively discussions. Mr. and Mrs. Earhart expected the girls to have opinions of their own. Should saloons be outlawed? Why, or why not? Was President Taft right to try to bust the trusts like American Tobacco and Standard Oil? Should women have the vote? Millie and Pidge thought they should.

"But we don't have to wait to get the vote before we work on elections," Millie pointed out. "We can campaign for Miss De Jarnette." Miss De Jarnette, Pidge's teacher, was running for superintendent of schools. The girls made a large cardboard sign in block letters: DOWN WITH THE MAN! UP WITH THE LADY . . . MISS DE JARNETTE OF COURSE, and they marched around the school yard with it. They were so proud when their candidate won.

The Earharts discussed books as well as current events, because they all loved to read. The most exciting present Mr. Earhart ever brought home from a trip was a complete set of Rudyard Kipling's works. It was a present for Mrs. Earhart, but Millie and Pidge were just as delighted when she opened the box and lifted out book after book: *Kim, The Jungle Book, Captains Courageous,* and on and on. "Leather bound!" exclaimed Amy Earhart. "You shouldn't have, Edwin."

Weeks later, Millie and Pidge were on the front porch when a collector came to ask for the first installment payment on the Kipling set. Millie saw a surprised, hurt look cross her mother's face, then disappear. "Isn't that like your father?" Mrs. Earhart remarked brightly as she went to get her purse. "So thoughtful, so generous—and so impractical!" She made all the payments from her housekeeping money.

Before long, Mr. Earhart was promoted to head of the claims office for the Rock Island Railroad Line. Now he was an important man in the company, with his name on the stationery letterhead. His salary was doubled.

Not only that, but Edwin Earhart was given a private railroad car for his business trips.

Sometimes he took Millie and Pidge out of school, and the whole family traveled to Missouri or Minnesota. Once they went as far as California. The private car had berths that folded down for sleeping, and its own little kitchen—and even a cook who traveled with them.

Millie had never seen Mother looking prouder of Dad than the time they visited Atchison in his private railroad car. First, the girls were allowed to invite four friends to lunch on the car. Millie and Pidge exchanged glances as the Atchison girls and boys gazed around the car. It was as if the Earhart girls had a fancy playhouse on wheels. After the cook served them lamb chops with little paper frills and rice and a special molded dessert, Mr. Earhart arranged for the young people to be pulled to Fort Leavenworth and back by a local train.

That evening, the Earharts welcomed Grandma and Grandpa to dinner on the car. During the elegant meal, Amy Earhart beamed across the table at her parents. It seemed to Millie that her mother was saying silently, *You see? I made the right choice of a husband, after all.* Edwin Earhart's in-laws could no longer criticize him for not being a "good provider."

Two years before they moved to Des Moines, the Earharts had started spending a month each summer in Minnesota, where it was cooler than in Kansas. They went to Lake Okabena in Worthington, where they roomed with the Manns, a farm family. The Manns had a girl named Genevieve, an older boy named Clinton, and several other children. Millie and Pidge pitched in to help with the farmwork, like herding the cows and haying. But they also had plenty of time for swimming, fishing, and—best of all—riding.

The Manns kept an Indian pony, Prince. The children rode him bareback, and sometimes "riding" included walking home.

Prince was a wily old animal, with tricks like scraping his rider off against an apple tree. But Millie took his mischief as a challenge. She made special pony treats of fresh grass and sugar cookies to bribe him.

At the lake Millie also spent time thinking about the way living things were put together. Sometimes, sitting on the shore of the lake, she would watch dragonflies dart over the water. They were so beautiful, shimmering green or blue, with wings like fairies. But these insects didn't just *look* beautiful— they flew beautifully, too. They could hang in the air, the way Millie could hang in the lake by treading water. Then they could zoom off in any direction.

In the Manns' pasture Millie found the scattered bones of several cows that had died in a blizzard, and she decided to put together one entire skeleton. She did a pretty good job, by checking the appearance of the live cows on the farm. But she had to give up when she got to the ribs—the Manns' cows were too well fed to count their ribs. Millie wanted to bring the bones back to Des Moines for further work, but Mother wouldn't allow it.

"How can I grow up to be a famous doctor like Colonel Gorgas in Panama, if you won't even let me study cow bones?" demanded Millie.

Amy Earhart smiled at her older daughter. "I'll be very proud of you when you do something as wonderful as Colonel Gorgas, fighting yellow fever and malaria. But you'll have to do it without these cow bones."

Every summer, visitors came to the lake: Uncle Carl and his new wife, cousins and friends from Atchison. Mr. Earhart himself came and went, because he couldn't take the whole month off from his job. But when he did join the family for a few days, they had more fun than ever.

One summer, on Genevieve Mann's birthday, the Earharts and Manns piled into automobiles and drove twenty miles on dirt roads to a picnic spot. Millie and Pidge had never ridden in a "horseless carriage" before. They sat in the front seat with Clinton Mann, watching fascinated as he swung the steering wheel around to pass a horse and wagon, or shifted gears to climb a hill. "Will we really get there in less than two hours?" shouted Millie over the roar and clatter.

"Sure thing," Clinton shouted back. "Why, *that's* not fast—an automobile on a race track can go faster than a mile a minute."

"A mile a minute," said Millie wonderingly. "Sixty miles an hour." Trains could run that fast, but they had to stick to their rails.

When they reached the picnic spot, Edwin Earhart showed the special hot-air balloons he had brought for the celebration. They all cheered as he inflated an eight-foot elephant and let it float off into the sky. The Earharts and the Manns sang "Happy Birthday" to Genevieve, and "In My Merry Oldsmobile," and "In the Good Old Summertime."

* * *

As Mr. Earhart prospered with the Rock Island Railroad, the family moved to bigger houses in better neighborhoods of Des Moines. On one move, Millie's cat, Von Sol (named after a grouchy character in a story), disappeared and had to be left behind. But Millie couldn't stand to think of her cat all alone, with night coming on. After supper, while Mr. and Mrs. Earhart were working to get their new home settled, she took a gunnysack and signaled Pidge with her eyes. When they had crept out the back door, Pidge whispered, "What are you doing?"

"Going to get Von Sol," said Millie. "Come on—you can help."

It was a long way to their old house on foot. But sure enough, there was a gray-and-white cat sitting on the doorstep. Taking one look at the gunnysack Millie held out, he ran up a birch tree near the porch.

"Silly Vonny," said Millie. She shinnied up

a post of the porch to the roof and climbed into the tree, making clucking noises to the cat. He hissed and laid back his ears, but in a few minutes she had stuffed him into the sack, and she climbed back down.

"It's dark," moaned Pidge as they started for home. "We didn't tell Mother and Dad where we were going. We're in trouble."

"I know," said Millie. "Don't worry, I'll say it was my fault. We *had* to rescue Von Sol." She would probably have to stay in after dinner for a week, but she would take her punishment without complaining.

The Earharts' last move in Des Moines was into a nice neighborhood near Drake University, where they had the chance to go to world-class concerts. On concert evenings, Amy Earhart might wear the violet silk dress that rustled as she walked, long kid gloves, and her sealskin fur coat. The girls, too, would wear high-necked silk dresses, and high-topped shoes that had to be buttoned with a button-hook. And Edwin Earhart was even more handsome than usual in his double-breasted coat with the long tails.

During the concerts Pidge would often fall asleep in her seat. But Millie listened with delight. She was musical, like her father. Back home, she and Dad would sit down at the piano and play by ear the opera melodies they had just heard.

The summer of 1911, when Millie turned fourteen, the Earharts went back to Lake Okabena once more. But now Millie sensed something wrong between her mother and father, like a chill fog blocking sunlight from the lake. One morning Mrs. Earhart did not appear at breakfast time, and Mr. Earhart came downstairs carrying his suitcases. "I'll need a ride to the station, Mann, if you can spare Clinton to drive me," he told the farmer.

"But, Dad, I thought you were staying all week," protested Pidge. "It's only Wednesday."

Millie was silent. She had woken up this morning to her mother's pleading and sobbing in the next bedroom. If Dad wouldn't listen to Mother, there was no use saying anything.

Mr. Earhart forced a smile and patted Pidge's head. "Isn't the railroad business rotten? I should have become a millionaire instead of a claims agent, and then I could stay with my girls all the time."

Later in the day, Mrs. Earhart talked to the girls about the sudden "long business trip" that had pulled Dad away from his vacation at the lake. Pidge seemed satisfied, and Millie pretended to believe it. With an effort she pushed what she really thought out of her mind. She would *not* let it spoil her summer.

This would be the Earharts' last summer at the lake.

Sad Grown-up Things

At the end of the summer of 1911, Mrs. Earhart took the girls to Atchison for a visit. Just as in past summers, Millie and Pidge played baseball and bicycled and traded books with their cousins and friends. Just as in past summers, Grandma's garden bloomed with red and pink spikes of gladioli, and the air was perfumed with heliotrope.

But it was impossible—impossible for Millie, at least—to ignore what the adults were talking about. She couldn't help seeing their tight lips and Mother's reddened eyes, and she couldn't help overhearing bits of strained discussions.

Grandma was not very well. Most mornings, she didn't sit in her usual place at the end of the breakfast table, pouring coffee and keeping an eye on the girls' table manners. Instead, the cook took a tray up to Grandma's bedroom.

Not only that, but Grandma was trying to persuade Mother to leave Dad. One morning, pausing in the upstairs hall outside her grandmother's bedroom, Millie heard Grandma speaking to Mother in a cold voice. She caught the words "drunkard" and "improvident"—and then "Edwin."

Grandma was talking about a disgraceful man who couldn't support his wife and daughters. She was talking about Dad. Grandma even offered to support the family herself, if Amy Earhart would divorce her husband.

Divorce. The word gave Millie a sick feeling. Nobody got divorced, at least nobody the Earharts and the Otises knew. It was shameful, not just for the husband and wife but for all their relatives.

Yet Grandma and Grandpa, who cared so much about being respectable, wanted their daughter to divorce their son-in-law. They must truly hate him. It was such a horrible thought that Millie didn't talk to anyone about it. It would have been comforting if Pidge had shown, just by a look or a word, that she knew, too. But Pidge was acting even younger than usual this summer, as if she was trying to squeeze back into the good old times.

That fall, back in Des Moines, the girls returned to school and Mr. Earhart returned home. Pidge still thought he had only been gone on a long business trip, and Millie tried to believe it. Maybe Grandma was wrong. Maybe the Earhart family was returning to normal.

One Saturday afternoon in September, Millie and Pidge and the other young people of the neighborhood sat on the Earharts' front lawn. No one wanted to miss playing Indians with Mr. Earhart. He would be home any minute from his half day at the office and change into old clothes. Then the whole gang would run howling after him, through the yard and into the barn.

A streetcar bell clanged. One of the boys exclaimed, "There's your father, Millie."

Millie glanced up the street. A man dressed in a business suit, carrying a briefcase, stepped down from the streetcar and began walking toward them. The boys and girls jumped up from the grass and ran to meet him, whooping.

But Millie hung back. This man's steps were slow and careful, unlike Dad's jaunty stride. "That's not my father," she called. "Let's go play football!"

The other children, who usually followed

her lead, paid her no attention. They knew that it *was* her father, and it was too late to pull them away. Mr. Earhart brushed through the cluster of boys and girls, not looking any of them in the eye. "Don' feel well," he said in a slurred voice. "Gotta lie down."

As he passed Millie, she smelled whiskey. She seemed to see him from a distance, as if he really were a stranger. *Why—Dad isn't any taller than I am*, she thought.

Edwin Earhart climbed the steps to the porch, wavering on the top step. Millie thought he would fall back and hit his head on the walk. But he righted himself and stumbled to the front door.

Mrs. Earhart opened the door with a welcoming smile. "Your Indian clothes are upstairs, Edwin." Millie watched helplessly as her mother's smile froze. Amy Earhart pulled her husband inside without another word.

As the door shut, Millie raised her chin and turned to face the neighborhood. But only Pidge's stunned, plump face looked back at her. The other girls and boys were turned away, scattering in different directions.

But they had seen the family's disgrace: Mr. Earhart coming home drunk in the middle of the day. Now everyone in the neighborhood knew what Millie and Mother and Pidge tried not to admit, even to themselves.

That winter, Grandma Amelia Otis died. It was so sad and strange for Millie, making the last trip to the house on the bluffs in Atchison for the funeral. This was the biggest family gathering Millie could remember, but also the quietest, with everyone talking in hushed tones. And Grandma, who had brought Millie up in this house on the Missouri River, and brought Mother up in the same house years before, and had lived here since the time when buffalo ran along the railroad tracks—Grandma was just not there anymore.

Within a few months Grandpa Otis had died, too. In May 1912 his will was read and the terms were published in the *Atchison Globe.* It was a nasty shock for the Earharts.

Amy Earhart's parents had left her a large sum of money, but she couldn't have it yet. Her parents had decided to leave it to her in a trust, to be managed by her older brother, Mark. Everyone in Atchison knew why: Judge and Mrs. Otis had been afraid Edwin Earhart would waste his wife's money.

The Earhart girls learned to avoid their father, especially in the evening. Instead of lingering at the dinner table for family discussions, Millie and Pidge would eat quickly, mumble something about homework, and disappear to their rooms. But even through closed doors, they could hear Dad going on downstairs.

"So Judge and Mrs. Alfred Otis didn't

think I could manage their little girl's money," he would say in a sarcastic, slurred voice. "The poor farmer's son wasn't good enough to marry Amy *Otis* in the first place. Her mother was a Harres of Philadelphia, you know."

Around their friends and neighbors, Millie and Pidge acted as if everything were fine. There was a lot of talk in Des Moines about how a national law ought to be passed against alcohol. Iowa had been a "dry" state for years, but somehow the bottles got smuggled in from other parts of the country. The minister of the Earharts' church praised the Prohibition movement in his sermons, and there were temperance rallies at the nearby university.

That fall, Mr. Earhart's manager found him drinking in the office. He put another man in charge of the Des Moines office and sent Edwin to a special hospital for a cure. "After he comes back," Amy Earhart assured the girls, "he'll be our own dear dad again."

It was awful that Dad had to be sent away, but Millie was relieved that the worst had finally happened. Mother looked hopeful now, and she saved money from the household budget to buy Dad a carpenter's bench and new tool set. "If he's busy and happy, he won't want that dreadful liquor any longer."

That made sense to Millie. She and Pidge worked for a neighbor, picking cherries in the hot sun, and earned three dollars. They bought Dad a jointed fishing pole with a reel on the handle.

When Edwin Earhart returned home a month later, clear eyed and cheerful, it seemed that Mother was right. Millie and Pidge laughed and clapped, watching their father waltz their mother around the kitchen. He hugged the girls and exclaimed over the carpenter's bench and the new fishing rod. "We'll catch us a whole string of perch on

Sunday. Monday, I'll be back at work, a new man, headed straight for the top—the main office in Chicago!"

But within a week or so, Edwin Earhart was drinking again. He never got back his old job as head of the Des Moines claims office. No one else would hire him, and he was out of work for almost a year. The Shedds, good friends who lived in Chicago now, invited Amy and the girls to come live with them—"until Edwin gets back on his feet." That would have meant splitting up the family, though, and Mrs. Earhart refused.

In the summer of 1913, Mr. Earhart finally got a filing clerk's job at a railway freight office in St. Paul, Minnesota. For a lawyer who had been head of the claims department for the Rock Island Railroad, it was a big comedown. But it was a job.

"St. Paul will be lovely," Mrs. Earhart assured the girls as they packed. "My uncle Charles Otis—you remember him from

Grandpa's funeral—is *somebody* in St. Paul society. And he's a dear man. When he takes us up, there'll be skating parties this winter— all sorts of fun."

Money Troubles

The Earharts moved into a big drafty house in a run-down section of St. Paul. They could barely pay the rent. Mrs. Earhart advertised for boarders, but no one turned up.

Millie and Pidge missed their friends in Des Moines. "Have you heard from Uncle Charles yet, Mother?" Pidge asked one day after school. "It'll be cold enough for skating pretty soon."

The very next day, Uncle Charles and his daughter, Marabel, who kept house for him, paid a visit to Amy Earhart. "We had such a nice chat over tea," Amy told the girls later.

"Skating parties next!" exclaimed Pidge. But Millie thought their mother's smile was strained, and she wondered if it had really been such a nice chat. Millie looked around the cold, shabby living room, and she imagined Cousin Marabel sipping tea and turning up her nose.

Uncle Charles never even invited the Earharts to dinner, let alone included them in skating parties at his private club. Amy Earhart did not know it, but her own brother, Mark, had hinted to their uncle that she was careless with money, undeserving, and disloyal to the Otis family. Mark had advised Uncle Charles not to get socially involved with the Earharts.

Millie knew her mother was miserable, but she wanted to enjoy her new life in St. Paul anyway. She liked St. Paul Central High School, which offered sports for girls as well as boys. Millie played on the basketball team.

She did well in her classes, too, including mathematics, physics, German, and Latin.

The Earharts joined the Episcopal church in their neighborhood, and the girls made friends through the youth group. Millie sang in the choir. That Christmas season, Millie and Pidge looked forward to a dance at the church. Boys had invited them, but it was the custom for girls to be escorted to a dance by their fathers. After the dance, the boys would walk the girls home, and be invited in for cocoa.

With excitement Millie and Pidge decorated the house that afternoon, got dressed in their party clothes, and waited in the living room for their father to come home from the office. His supper was waiting in the oven, but Mr. Earhart did not appear. The clock in the living room ticked off the passing time.

"Dad won't have time to eat his supper now," said Millie finally. "Or take his bath. He'll just have time to change his clothes."

A little later, Pidge spoke up. "We should be leaving right now, if we're going to get to the church hall before the band strikes up."

Still later, Millie forced a smile for her sister and said, "We'll be fashionably late, I guess. We'll miss a few dances, but we can still have a good time."

Finally it was too late for them to go to the dance at all. Millie paced the front hall, trying out excuses to tell the boys who had expected them at the dance. How could Dad do this to her?

At nine o'clock Mr. Earhart stumbled in the door, trying to make a joke of it. He swept off his hat in a drunken imitation of a gallant gentleman. "Didja think I'd be late t' th' ball?"

Pidge burst into tears and ran up the stairs, but Millie felt cold and hard inside. She didn't speak to her father. With a swish of her party skirt, she stalked into the living room. She pulled down the decorations, turned out the

light, and then climbed the stairs to the girls'
bedroom.

Pidge had cried herself to sleep, but Millie
lay awake, trying to read. Instead, she found
herself staring at the bare branches lit by the
street lamp outside the window. *When I'm
grown up*, Millie thought, *I will never let
myself get stuck the way Mother is stuck.*

Throughout the spring in St. Paul, Millie
and Pidge grew closer in a sad conspiracy.
Their goals were to make things easier on
their mother, and to never let anyone outside
the family know about "Dad's sickness."

One bitterly cold day in February, the sisters walked for miles to buy groceries at a
bargain store. "If we can get a leg of lamb for
eighty-five cents," Millie figured, "we'll save
money *and* have a nickel apiece left over for
streetcar fare." But at the store, they couldn't
seem to find a leg of lamb small enough for
their budget.

The butcher ran out of patience, weighing every leg of lamb in the case, and finally Millie settled for one that cost ninety-six cents. "I've got a penny in my pocket," she whispered to her sister. "You can ride home on the streetcar with the bundles, and I'll walk."

At the streetcar stop, Millie gave Pidge the four cents change and then fumbled with stiff fingers for the coin in her pocket. "Oh, hooray, it isn't a penny—it's a token! If only I had a penny, too, we could both—"

"Millie," Pidge interrupted, "it's a *Des Moines* token."

Millie looked again. Pidge was right. For a moment, Millie wished with all her heart that they were back in Des Moines, in the days before Dad started drinking.

A streetcar pulled up with a clang, and the other passengers climbed in. But the Earhart girls had to trudge all the way home again, lugging the groceries, in the icy wind.

That year, the girls sewed their own Easter outfits. They didn't have the money to buy cloth, but they used some silk curtains left over from better times in Des Moines. They dyed some of the silk green for Pidge's skirt and some of it brown for Millie's. On Easter, the Earhart sisters managed to look just as fashionable as any of their friends.

While Millie was scrimping in St. Paul, she wrote cheerful letters to her old friend Ginger Park in Atchison. They would both be high school seniors next year, and they both planned to go to Bryn Mawr College in Pennsylvania after they graduated. "I'm going if I have to drive a grocery wagon to accumulate the cash," wrote Millie.

But it wasn't easy to stay cheerful and make the best of things. One evening Mr. Earhart, coming home in a stupor, stumbled into the path of an automobile. He wasn't badly hurt, but he had to have stitches at a hospital—for ten precious dollars. Afterward, he promised to quit drinking, but the girls didn't get their hopes up. At school, Millie couldn't seem to concentrate as well, and her grade average slipped from an A- to a B.

Mrs. Earhart grew more and more nervous and exhausted. She would jump at ordinary noises, such as Millie dropping her schoolbooks on the kitchen table. One day the girls came home to find her sitting on the stairs, shivering so hard that she couldn't stand up for several minutes. The next afternoon, Millie went down the street to ask the family doctor what to do.

The doctor looked at Millie over his glasses for a moment. Then he said, "I'll be frank with you. Mrs. Earhart is on the point of a nervous breakdown. You make your mother quit worrying and rest flat on her bed at least three hours a day."

In the summer of 1914, Edwin Earhart decided to take the family to Springfield, Missouri, where he thought he had been offered a better job. Once more, the girls helped Mrs. Earhart wrap the china in newspaper and pack it in barrels. Then they set out on the seven-hour journey from Minnesota to Missouri in a crowded, noisy day coach. It was hot, although the windows of the train were open, and soot from the smokestack powdered their clothes and faces.

Millie didn't complain, but she couldn't help remembering the private car the Earharts used to travel in. There was a snapshot in their photograph album, taken when Millie was thirteen, of her and Pidge and Dad smiling from the platform at the back of the car. Millie remembered crawling into her snug upper berth, which the porter had made up with one corner of the white sheet turned neatly down. She would drift off to sleep, in those days, listening to the rhythm of the train wheels.

These days were even worse than Millie

realized. When they reached Springfield, Mr. Earhart went to the railroad office—and came back flushed with anger. "Cheats! Liars!" There had been a misunderstanding. There was no permanent job for him in Springfield, after all.

The family stood in the little park by the railroad station, trying to take in this bad news. Millie glanced at Pidge, and she knew that she and her sister were thinking the same bitter thought at their father. *Just when we were starting to feel at home in St. Paul, you dragged us away—for this.*

Mrs. Earhart spoke up quickly, as if she was afraid Millie would say her thoughts out loud. Her voice shook only a little as she said, "Well, I think this is our chance to take the Shedds up on their very gracious offer. You know they wanted us to come to them last year, and they were so disappointed when I said no. Yes, I think it would be best for the girls and me to go stay with the Shedds in

Chicago. Just until you get back on your feet, Edwin."

"How could you think of walking out on me, Amy?" exclaimed Mr. Earhart. "The girls don't want to desert their poor father. Do you, Millie? Pidge?"

Pidge turned to Millie. Millie, now almost seventeen, gave her father a level look. A few years ago, she would have been clasping his arm to comfort him, gazing reproachfully at her mother. She would have been shaking her fist at the railway office, because the company hadn't told him the job had fallen through.

Millie turned her gaze on her mother. If Mother was close to a nervous breakdown, as the doctor had said, this might put her over the edge. "I think we ought to go to Chicago," said Millie firmly.

"So do I," Pidge agreed. "Just for a while, Dad."

The family was splitting up.

Amelia Takes Charge

Mrs. Earhart and Pidge moved to Chicago, where the Shedds were delighted to have them. A few years ago, Edwin Earhart had helped Mr. Shedd get a job in Des Moines, and the Shedds had stayed with the Earharts while they were looking for a house. Now the Shedds were glad to repay the kindness. Meanwhile, Mr. Earhart moved to Kansas City, Missouri. There he lived with his widowed sister and tried to build up a law practice.

Amelia would join her mother and sister in Chicago, but first she spent a month in Atchison. She stayed with the Challisses: Aunt Rilla, Uncle James, and the cousins Toot, Katch, Jack, and baby Peggy.

"This will be your room while you're with us, dear." Aunt Rilla showed Amelia to the bedroom where Toot and Katch's nanny used to live in the old days. A warm breeze fluttered the starched curtains, and the room was scented with a bouquet of rose geraniums on the dresser. At the Challisses, at least, everything was the way it ought to be. Amelia unpacked her trunk and then ran over to Ginger Park's to say hello.

Of course Grandma's house was right next door to the Challisses', a reminder of the days when Amelia had two happy homes: her grandmother's in Atchison and her parents' in Kansas City or Des Moines. Against those memories Amelia put up a fence in her mind, higher and blanker than the fence she had climbed over so many times.

No one in Atchison asked Amelia why the Earharts had left St. Paul, or why only Amy Earhart and the girls were moving to Chicago. No one even mentioned Edwin Earhart, and Amelia didn't mention Dad, either. Aunt Rilla, she realized, had never liked him. Uncle James, a lawyer like Dad, had enjoyed having a private drink with Edwin and telling stories and laughing. But he had never wanted him as a business partner in his law firm.

During her month in Atchison, Amelia acted as if everything were just fine with the Earharts. She swam, she played tennis, she read, she played card games. In the evening she and Toot might go to a party, or they might sit on the Challisses' porch and sing while Uncle James played his guitar. As long as she kept busy—laughing, talking, dancing, hitting the tennis ball right down the line— Amelia could believe that she still fit in with her cousins and Ginger and all the people she'd known since she was a baby.

It was a little hard when the girls Amelia's age talked about their plans for next year, after high school. Toot was going to Wheaton College, near Chicago. Ginger was going to Bryn Mawr, as she had decided years ago. Toot and Ginger's fathers could afford to send them to private colleges, while Amelia's father couldn't even pay the rent. But Amelia didn't hint at this, and neither did her friends.

In September, Amelia packed her trunk again and rode the train from Atchison to Chicago. Mother and Pidge were still living with the Shedds, in the Morgan Park district of Chicago, and they were looking for an apartment nearby. "It'll be so comfortable to be close to our friends," explained Amy Earhart. "And how nice for Pidge, to be enrolled at the high school with Elizabeth Shedd."

But after one tour of the Morgan Park high school, Amelia had different ideas. She still intended to *do* something with her life, and she wanted the best education possible. "The chemistry lab at this school is no better than a kitchen sink," she said. "Hyde Park High School is the best in Chicago, and this is my senior year. So we need to live in Hyde Park."

Mrs. Earhart tried to talk her out of it, but in the end, they moved to Hyde Park. It was a more expensive neighborhood than Morgan Park, and the only lodgings they could afford there were rooms in someone else's apartment.

Hyde Park High School *was* the best public school in Chicago. Besides a good education, it offered all kinds of sports and clubs. But this year Amelia didn't play basketball or baseball, and she didn't join the drama club or the choral society.

Amelia didn't make any friends in Chicago. Each day after school, she went straight home to the little apartment that she and Mother and Pidge shared with two unpleasant landladies. These women were so stingy that they tried to discourage the Earharts from using the living room. When they left for work each day, they would turn the chairs upside down and drape sheets over the rest of the furniture.

Poor Mother! Amelia knew that Amy Earhart was miserable here. The only way she could try to make up for it was to keep her mother company.

In the spring of 1915 the *Aitchpe*, the Hyde Park High School yearbook, came out. Amelia didn't buy one, but she glanced through a classmate's copy. There was her senior picture, looking pretty in a blank kind of way. She wore a ribbon around her neck and her fair hair was piled on top of her head. The caption was a quotation: "Meek loveliness is 'round thee spread."

"Meek loveliness!" Amelia would have

laughed out loud, if she had felt like laughing. Her classmates didn't know the first thing about Amelia Earhart. Well, that was just the way she wanted it. In June, Amelia didn't attend graduation or even pick up her diploma.

Now Toot Challis would be getting ready to go to Wheaton College, Amelia knew. Ginger Park was taking this year off from school, but without a doubt, next summer she would be packing for Bryn Mawr. As for Amelia, how would *she* ever get to college? It looked as if her joke to Ginger about driving a grocery wagon was no joke.

There was one bright spot in the Earharts' life: Edwin Earhart was sober again. Amy and the girls left Chicago and went to live with him in Kansas City, Missouri, where he was running a small law office. They would never again be the happy, lucky family they had been in Des Moines, but they were grateful just to have a house to themselves.

And now, maybe there was a way to get money for the girls' education. Together Edwin and Amy began to fight the terms of her parents' will, which had left her inheritance in a trust managed by her brother, Mark. After a long struggle, the courts granted Amy full control of her money.

Now that she could afford it, Mrs. Earhart decided to send Amelia to the exclusive Ogontz School, a society finishing school in Philadelphia. Like her mother, Amy Earhart had always been concerned with social position. She had been humiliated for her daughters as well as herself during the years in St. Paul and Chicago, when she had no social standing at all.

Amelia didn't care about being "finished" socially, but she let her mother decide on the school this time. The next year, she could join Ginger at Bryn Mawr. The important thing was, she *was* going away to school! In the fall of 1916, as the train carried her east, away from her family and their problems, Amelia felt her spirits lift.

Luckily, Ogontz was a good place to get an all-around education, as well as social polish. Amelia, now nineteen, happily threw herself into all kinds of activities. "I played hockey yesterday and made two goals, the only ones made," she bragged in a letter to her mother that October. She also enjoyed horseback riding, going to concerts, plays, and lectures in Philadelphia, and student clubs.

Digging into her schoolwork, Amelia soon had a reputation as a thoughtful, serious student. "Amelia was always pushing into unknown seas in her thinking, her reading, and in experiments in science," as the headmistress, Miss Sutherland, put it. "Her most vivid characteristic was her intellectual curiosity."

One of the best things about Ogontz was that Amelia's Aunt Margaret, her mother's sister, lived only a few miles away. Rather than going home to Kansas City, Amelia spent most of her vacations with the Balises, Aunt Margaret's happy family.

In letters to her mother Amelia complained about Ogontz's strict rules, although they were typical for a girls' boarding school in those days. If the students went into Philadelphia to a concert or the theater, they must have an adult chaperon. Amelia had to get written permission from her mother in order to go to a football game with her roommate and her roommate's father. The girls were not allowed to play their Victrolas (early windup record players) in their rooms, because the dormitory should not sound like a "beer garden."

But these rules didn't seem to cramp Amelia's high spirits, any more than her grandmother's rules had in her Atchison home. In the safe setting of Ogontz, she felt like her playful younger self again. She and her friends gave each other teasing nicknames—tall, thin

Amelia's was "Butterball." One of her favorite pranks was climbing on the dormitory roof in her nightgown. More than once, she was caught up there and her Aunt Margaret was called by the Ogontz School authorities.

During the summer of 1917, Amelia continued to enjoy herself. Although she visited her family in Kansas City, she spent a good part of the summer with friends at a camp on Lake Michigan. In letters home she mentioned swimming, canoeing, hiking, playing tennis, and some young men who were especially nice to her. She was impressed with a boy of twenty-three, the son of one of Theodore Roosevelt's Rough Riders. He "was offered a position as war photographer but refused it to go into the aviation corps," she wrote her mother.

The U. S. Army had an aviation corps, because flying machines had made great progress since 1908, when Amelia saw the comical contraption at the Iowa State Fair.

Now they could fly far enough and fast enough to spy and to drop bombs. Ever since World War I broke out in Europe in 1914, both sides had been using aircraft. In April 1917 the United States joined the war with their own fleet of airplanes.

The girls at Ogontz were caught up in the patriotic spirit that swept the country. By October, Amelia and her roommate, Eleanor, were leaders in the student Red Cross chapter. The girls raised money to buy Liberty Bonds to support the war effort, and they knit khaki-colored sweaters for the Allied soldiers. Amelia and Eleanor also took a Red Cross course in surgical dressings.

In Amelia's letters to her mother that fall, her news about the war effort was mixed up with reports on the battle over sororities (private social clubs) at Ogontz. The headmistress had decided to abolish sororities, and Amelia was one of the few students who agreed with her. Maybe Amelia thought of her lonely year in Chicago, when she had kept to herself and belonged to nothing. Many of the Ogontz sorority girls were angry with Amelia for criticizing them, and she was upset at the danger of losing their friendship. But that didn't change her mind about what she thought was right.

In the midst of her busy life at school, Amelia was aware that her parents were not happy. That October she wrote her mother: "I have awful twinges of conscience about leaving you to your silent severity (your description)." Amy finally left Edwin and Kansas City and moved to an apartment in Toronto, Canada. There Muriel was starting at St. Margaret's, a college preparatory school.

Mrs. Earhart's unhappy marriage made Amelia think more about the kind of life *she* intended to lead. Before her marriage, Amy Otis had wanted to go to Vassar College, but her father would not allow it. Her sister, Amelia's Aunt Margaret, had longed to go to medical school at Cornell. But again, Alfred Otis would not hear of it.

Amelia was determined that *she* would lead a life of achievement in the world, whether or not she ever got married and raised a family. She kept a scrapbook titled "Activities of Women," pasting in newspaper and magazine clippings about women who impressed her. One was a fire lookout, working in South Dakota for the Federal Forestry Service. Another was a film producer, another the president of a county medical society, and another an industrial psychologist.

For Christmas vacation that year, 1917, Amelia joined her mother and sister in Toronto. She was happy to be with her family, but she was shocked at the sight of all the wounded and disabled soldiers on the streets. The Canadians, along with the rest of the

British Empire, had been at war with Germany since 1914. "For the first time I realized what the World War meant," Amelia wrote later. "Instead of new uniforms and brass bands, I saw only the results of a desperate four years' struggle; men without arms and legs, men who were paralyzed and men who were blind."

Suddenly Amelia's student life seemed childish, and she decided to drop out of school and volunteer as a nurse's aide. "I can't bear the thought of going back to school and being so useless," she told her mother.

"That means giving up graduating," protested Mrs. Earhart.

But Amelia was determined. Later in life she explained, "Returning to school was impossible, if there was work that I could do."

"Work That I Could Do"

So Amelia stayed in Canada instead of returning to school. She and Muriel moved into an apartment at the St. Regis Hotel. Muriel went on with her studies at St. Margaret's, while Amelia enrolled in nursing courses.

With all the wounded soldiers returning from the war, there was a great need for nurses. Before long, Amelia was working as a nurse's aide at Spadina Military Hospital in

Toronto. She was a naturally good nurse, like her great-grandmother Maria Harres. She was not put off by seeing sick and suffering people up close. Strong and energetic, she cheerfully made beds, carried trays, and rubbed patients' backs. Sometimes she drove the light trucks that brought supplies to the hospital. She also helped in the hospital laboratory, and in the kitchen.

Amelia believed that the soldiers would recover faster if she could raise their spirits, and she found little ways to cheer them up. For instance, they obviously hated the rice pudding the hospital served night after night for dessert. One patient expressed his feelings by shaping his serving of pudding into a mound like a grave. He formed the letters R.I.P ("rest in peace") on it with matchsticks.

Amelia persuaded the hospital to serve blanc mange, a tastier pudding, and she stayed up late, making the first batch herself. The next day, clearing trays, she found all the dessert plates empty. On one plate there was a cheer for her, the only American nurse's aide, spelled out in matchsticks:

RAY RAY
U.S.A.

Although she was working ten-hour shifts at the hospital, Amelia still had energy left over. When she and Muriel both had a Saturday free, they would head for the stable and go riding together. The horse that interested Amelia the most was a big dappled gray.

"I don't think you'd better try to ride him, miss," the groom warned her. "He's named Dynamite. He must have gotten some pretty mean treatment. He tossed off two of the boys who tried to ride him yesterday."

I'll bet I can change his mind, thought Amelia. She began stopping by the stable every day after work to bring apples to Dynamite and talk to him. Within a month, she was riding him without any trouble, and he was safe for other riders, too.

Amelia's handling of Dynamite impressed some Canadian air force officers who rode at the stable. They invited her and Muriel to the airfield to watch the airplanes take off and land. Gazing at the new military aircraft swooping across the sky, Amelia was amazed.

Amelia had not thought much about airplanes since the Earharts' visit to the state fair in Des Moines, ten years ago. But these airplanes were no clumsy "flying machines." They were like—why, they were like great birds. They reminded her of the hawks she used to watch from the bluffs over the Missouri River.

Immediately Amelia wanted to fly herself, but non-soldiers were not allowed in the planes. She came back to the field again and again, anyway. She liked to stand very close as the planes took off on their skis, so that the snow blown back by the propellers stung her face.

Some of Amelia's patients at the hospital

were pilots. She listened to their stories of being shot down over enemy territory, or of crashing during training flights. She could imagine herself up in the sky, with danger all around—lonely, but filled with a wild, free joy.

In the summer of 1918, World War I was winding to a close. At the same time, a great influenza epidemic swept through the United States and Canada. This disease was as deadly as the war, slaughtering thousands. Now Amelia worked twelve- and fourteen-hour shifts in the pneumonia ward of the hospital, ladling medicine out of a bucket.

Amelia was an unusually healthy person, but finally in November she came down with influenza, too. She was sick for weeks, and then she developed a sinus infection. Her face hurt, and it was hard to breathe through her nose. At that time the only treatment for sinusitis was surgery.

After her operation, Amelia was in pain,

and much too weak to work. To her disgust, the doctors ordered her to take it easy for the rest of the spring of 1919. By this time Muriel and Mrs. Earhart were living in Northampton, Massachusetts, while Muriel studied for the entrance exams for Smith College.

Amelia joined her mother and sister and tried not to do much of anything. But she thought the small New England village of Northampton was boring, and her spirits sank. To keep busy, she signed up for a class in repairing automobile engines. It was fun to find out how things worked, and who knew—the skill might come in handy some day.

That summer Mrs. Earhart decided to take the girls on a vacation. Amelia found a cottage for them at Lake George, in upstate New York. By then Amelia was nearly well, and she could swim and canoe with Muriel and the other young people at the lake.

A tall, slim girl with dark blond hair down

to her waist, Amelia attracted boys easily. Frank Stabler, the young man in the cottage across the road, had quite a crush on her, as his sister Marian informed Amelia. Amelia enjoyed sports and dancing and discussions with boys, but she wasn't inclined to fall in love with anyone.

Amelia was twenty-two, and she wanted to decide what to do with her life. She'd already thought about becoming a doctor, and her nursing work in Toronto had made her even more interested in medicine than before. While the Earharts were at Lake George, Aunt Margaret visited. She must have encouraged Amelia to go to medical school—as Alfred Otis had not allowed Margaret to do.

In the fall, when Muriel entered Smith College, Amelia enrolled in premed courses at Columbia University in New York City. Her mother traveled to New York to get her settled in, and Amy Earhart fretted about leaving her daughter alone in the city. But

Amelia rented an apartment on Morningside Drive and plunged into her classes. *"Don't worry,"* she wrote her mother.

At Columbia, Amelia became good friends with Louise De Schweinitz, a graduate of Smith College. Louise also intended to become a doctor, and the girls found themselves in the same science classes. Together they studied hard, and read poetry. They perched on stools at the drugstore counter that was a student hangout, and discussed things seriously and joked over mugs of cocoa. They went for hikes and picnics on the Palisades, across the Hudson River from Columbia.

Adventurous Amelia got Louise to help her explore the tunnels connecting the Columbia buildings, and once they climbed into the lap of the statue in front of the university library and sat there eating cherries. One day during the spring of 1920, Amelia persuaded Louise to climb with her to the top of the library. Louise took a picture of Amelia perched on top of the dome, hugging her knees and looking pleased with herself.

The professor of Amelia and Louise's elementary biology and zoology class was impressed with both girls, but especially with Amelia. Often after laboratory sessions he would invite both of them to tea, brewed in a beaker over a Bunsen burner. He thought Amelia had the ideal mind—sharp, logical, inquiring—to become a research scientist.

By the end of the spring term, Amelia had a B+ average for the year, and seemingly she was happy in New York. But family responsibilities were pulling at Amelia again. Her father, now sober for good, had moved to Los Angeles and set up a law practice there. He wanted the whole family together again, in California. During the spring Mrs. Earhart joined him, trying once again to make their marriage work. They both wrote Amelia, pleading for her to come west and live with them.

Amelia felt she ought to try to shore up her parents' shaky marriage, so she quit Columbia and moved to Los Angeles. She had some idea that she could continue her studies in medical research in California. And she wondered if she was cut out to be a doctor, after all. Anyway, she couldn't ignore her mother's pleas.

"I'll see what I can do to keep Mother and Dad together, Pidge," Amelia told Muriel as she boarded the train for the West Coast. "But after that I'm going to come back here and live my own life."

Amelia arrived in Los Angeles in the summer of 1920 and settled in with her parents on West Twenty-third Street. Soon afterward, she got her father to take her to an air meet in nearby Long Beach. Southern California, a warm, dry place with plenty of open land, was ideal for flying, and the aviation business was booming. The movie industry in Hollywood made films about heroic pilots, and actors went up in planes as a way to get publicity. Cecil B. DeMille, a famous studio head, even had his own airfield off Wilshire Boulevard.

Besides the new aircraft being built, there were many planes left over from World War I. The common military training plane was the biplane Curtiss JN-4, or Jenny, and the Canuck, the Canadian version of the Jenny. These had two open cockpits and a wingspan of forty-four feet. Their two sets of wings, one above and one below the body of the aircraft, were covered with canvas. They could fly as fast as seventy-five miles per hour, and go one hundred miles before refueling.

About this time, the U. S. Post Office began using planes to deliver mail. In the fall of 1920, post office planes set a new record for New York to San Francisco service—only seventy-eight hours. The fastest trains took one hundred hours to cover the same distance.

The post office flew war surplus DH-4s, more reliable than the Jenny. Still, the flying was dangerous. The instruments in planes at that time were unreliable, and it was very unsafe to fly at night. Pilots had to use road maps for navigation, flying low to find landmarks such as a church steeple or a railroad crossing. Of the first forty pilots hired by the Air Mail Service, all except nine died. Charles Lindbergh was one of the nine survivors.

Airplanes were such a novelty that some pilots earned a living doing stunts for crowds and taking up passengers for short flights. The most famous woman pilot, or "aviatrix" as women pilots were called then, was Laura Bromwell. That spring, as Amelia knew, Bromwell had crashed to her death while performing a loop-the-loop. The first stunt flier for the movies, Owen Locklear, had also been killed that spring, doing a tailspin.

But danger had never bothered Amelia. Every chance she got, she went to air meets. She watched the planes roar down the runway in clouds of dust, lift off, and rise until they were dots in the sky. With every meet, she became more determined to go up in the air herself. That December, Edwin Earhart paid ten dollars for Amelia to take a ten-minute airplane ride from Rogers Field, off Wilshire Boulevard.

This "airport," like all the airfields of that time, was only a wide stretch of dirt—there were no paved runways. The craft for Amelia's first flight was a biplane with two open cockpits, probably a Canuck or Jenny. The pilot, Frank Wright, was an experienced flyer, but Amelia did not think much of his attitude. He seemed to be worried that just because she was a woman, she would panic and try to jump out of the plane.

Amelia, wearing a borrowed leather helmet and goggles, climbed into the forward cockpit. She felt the plane tremble as the engine roared. Attendants pulled away the wheel chocks, and the plane rolled forward.

Faster and faster the plane bumped over the dirt field. Waiting eagerly for liftoff, Amelia didn't notice anything in the first moment, except that the jolting stopped. Then she realized that the ground was dropping away.

I am flying, thought Amelia.

The day was clear and sunny, like almost all the days in southern California. Amelia gazed down on the oil wells near Wilshire Boulevard, then down on the city of Los Angeles, surrounded by orange groves. Beetlelike automobiles crawled along the highways. As the plane circled higher and higher, she could see over the western hills to the Pacific Ocean.

Amelia knew they must be going fast, but it didn't seem that way. There was nothing up in the air to mark the speed, like the telegraph poles flicking past the window of a

130

train or an automobile. They seemed to be gliding slowly over a huge relief map.

I am going to learn to fly myself, thought Amelia.

California Flying

At dinner that night Amelia said to her parents, "I think I'd like to learn to fly." To her, this was a huge understatement. She thought she would *die* if she couldn't learn to fly.

"Not a bad idea," her father teased. "When do you start?"

"Yes, why should the Hollywood starlets have all the fun?" said her mother.

Amelia smiled, but she was already considering where she would take her lessons. She would *not* learn from Frank Wright. She'd heard there was a woman instructor at the Kinner Air Field.

The joke was on Edwin Earhart a few days later, when Amelia announced that she had signed up for lessons: five hundred dollars for twelve hours. "I can't pay for them," her father protested. "How could you imagine I could afford five hundred dollars for flying lessons?"

"Besides, Millie, it's so dangerous," Amy Earhart put in. "Do you know how Will Rogers defines 'airfield'? 'A tract of land completely surrounded by high tension wires and high chimneys, adjacent to a cemetery.'"

"Will Rogers only talks like that because he's a humorist," said Amelia. "He flies, himself." She knew very well that flying wasn't exactly safe. She had taken a look at the owner's manual that Curtiss Aircraft gave out with the Jenny. "Never forget that the engine may stop, and at all times keep this in mind," it warned. But that didn't mean she shouldn't

133

learn to fly. It only meant she should learn to fly so well that she could make emergency landings.

If her father wouldn't pay for her lessons, Amelia would earn the money herself. She got a job with the telephone company, in the mailroom. She also worked for her father on Saturdays.

Kinner Field, where Amelia decided to take lessons, was a dirt strip bordered by vegetable fields off of Long Beach Boulevard, in the South Gate section of Los Angeles. Bert Kinner had put up a windsock and a small hangar, and there he was building his own plane, the Kinner Airster. A young woman pilot, Neta Snook, test-flew his planes in return for the space to give lessons.

Neta made Amelia smile. She was small and feisty, with bright red bobbed hair. The first time they met, Neta was wearing a grease-stained monkey suit. Amelia wore a well-cut brown suit with a silk scarf and gloves, and her long honey-colored hair was braided and coiled around her head.

The men at the airfield called Neta "Snooky" and pretended to think she was a boy. But Amelia admired Neta. She was only a year older than Amelia, but she'd focused all her energy on making a career for herself in flying. She was the first woman to graduate from the Curtiss School of Aviation, and she'd earned the money to buy and personally rebuild her own plane, a Canuck. Since then, she'd made her living as an aviator—flying passengers, giving lessons, and going up in the air with advertising signs on the bottom of her wings.

Early in January 1921, Amelia showed up at Kinner Field for her first lesson. She was dressed in riding pants and boots, the usual flying clothes for both men and women. Women didn't normally wear pants in those days, but they were the only practical clothes for flying. Getting into a plane was something like mounting a horse—you had to put one foot in a toehold on the side of the plane and swing the other leg up into the cockpit.

Every Saturday and Sunday, Amelia rode the streetcar all the way to the end of the line in South Gate, then walked the last few miles to Kinner Field. She progressed quickly from instruction on the ground to lessons in the air in Neta's Canuck. The plane had dual controls, with the teacher sitting in the back cockpit. There was a rudder bar, worked by the feet, to turn the plane. The stick, coming up from the floor, was pushed forward and back and from side to side to make the plane climb, dive, or tilt the wings one way or the other. There was no gas gauge to show how much fuel the plane had left, and no brakes to slow the plane on landing.

At the beginning of June, Muriel arrived from Massachusetts for the summer. Amelia met her at the train station. "Millie!" exclaimed Muriel as she hugged her sister.

"You bobbed your hair! What did Mother say? And look at all your freckles."

"I had to cut my hair, Pidge." Amelia grinned, wrinkling her sun-freckled nose. "As I told Mother, I decided the other day when I hitched a ride from the end of the streetcar line to the airfield. A little girl in the automobile— she reminded me a bit of Katch—said, 'You can't be an aviatrix, because you don't have bobbed hair.' So I had to cut it off, didn't I?"

Muriel didn't want to learn to fly, but it was fun for her to take part in Amelia's new life that summer. On weekends the girls rode the streetcar together and hitched rides to the hot, dusty airfield. They would bring a basket of sandwiches and one of Amy Earhart's chocolate cakes, and after Amelia's lesson they would picnic on the shady side of the hangar. Muriel learned to shellac the canvas wings of Neta's plane and to replace rusted guide wires.

By this time Amelia was determined to own her own plane. The cheapest choice would have been a used Canuck, like Neta's plane, but Amelia was impressed by Bert Kinner's Airster, a small biplane with an air-cooled engine. It was faster and easier to maneuver than the Canuck, and it was so light that she could lift it by the tail and move it around herself.

"You don't have no sense if you buy the Airster, Millie," Neta told her one day. The three young women were lounging in the shade of the hangar, out of the hot, dazzling sunlight. "You could get yourself a used Canuck, like mine, for less than one thousand dollars. Bert's asking two thousand dollars for his demonstration model!"

"The Airster has a stronger body, and it only weighs 600 pounds, to the Canuck's 1,430 pounds," Amelia pointed out. "It can fly twice as far, it can climb three thousand feet higher, and it goes up to ninety miles an hour. So who's got sense?" Amelia's tone was pleasant, but Muriel recognized a remote look in her sister's eyes. That look meant that Millie was going to do what *she* thought best.

To buy the Airster, Amelia used her own small savings, borrowed Muriel's savings, and worked long hours at the telephone company. Her mother could see that Amelia wanted this plane more than she had ever wanted anything in her life, and so she agreed to give her the rest of the money.

On July 24, Amelia's twenty-fourth birthday, Mrs. Earhart rode the streetcar with Amelia and Muriel to see the *Canary*, as Amelia had named her bright yellow plane. "Oh, Millie, I can understand why you wanted it so much." Mrs. Earhart reached up and patted the plane's nose, as if it were a pony.

"Don't you almost want to feed it apples?" Amelia beamed. "Bert Kinner is going to let me use his hangar and repair shop. And I'm going to let him use the *Canary* for sales demonstrations."

Amelia bought herself a leather helmet

and goggles and an aviator's leather jacket, which she slept in and rubbed grease into until the new look was gone. Her lessons with Neta continued in the Airster, and one day they flew to the nearby Goodyear field to see Donald Douglas's first airplane, the Cloudster. Taking off from Goodyear, the plane failed to gain enough height, and they were in danger of plowing into a grove of eucalyptus trees at the end of the runway.

Deliberately, Amelia stalled the engine to bring the plane down right away. The crash damaged the propeller and the landing gear, but Amelia coolly turned off the engine so there was no danger of fire. Neta twisted around in the forward cockpit. "Are you all right?" she started to call to Amelia. Then she exclaimed, "What are you doing?"

Amelia was peering into her compact mirror, powdering her nose. "We have to look nice when the reporters come," she explained. She had survived her first crash.

Soon Neta thought Amelia was ready to solo, but first Amelia wanted to learn to handle her plane in every possible situation. She switched instructors to take lessons in stunt flying from John Montijo, a veteran pilot of World War I. For months Amelia practiced banked turns, tailspins, loops, barrel rolls, and dives, until she was ready to recover the Airster from any unexpected position.

After all this preparation, Amelia wasn't even nervous during her solo flight. When she landed again, Neta and Muriel ran across the dirt strip to congratulate her. "You're a real pilot now, Millie!" called Muriel.

"Yeah, but I thought I taught you to land better than that," Neta teased her.

Pushing her goggles up on her head, Amelia gave them a rueful smile. "You did. That was a thoroughly rotten landing."

That fall, 1921, Amelia began to take part in air meets. Only a little over a year ago, she had been in the earthbound audience, looking on wistfully as the pilots flew off the field in a roar and a cloud of dust. Now she was the "lady pilot Miss Amelia Earhart," as *The Ace*, the foremost aviation magazine, called her. She was written up as an attraction at air rodeos, where she did stunt flying.

In those days, women who attempted such "male" activities as flying airplanes could expect to be criticized as "unfeminine." But not Amelia, who was slender, graceful, and naturally stylish. Amelia knew how good she looked, with her long legs, in riding pants or slacks. Her leather pilot's jacket was now properly creased and grease stained, and she curled her short blond hair to give it an attractively tousled look. Her appealing grin seemed to say to the crowds at air meets, "Flying's nothing to be afraid of—and it's great fun!"

While Amelia was becoming one of the best-known aviatrixes in California, Amy and

Edwin Earharts' marriage and money problems worsened. Edwin had given up alcohol for good, but he had become a Christian Scientist, and he and Amy had less and less in common. Edwin's law business was doing well enough, but as usual the Earharts were living beyond their means.

Trying to increase her income, Amy Earhart invested in a mine in Nevada owned by a friend of Amelia's. When the mine failed, early in 1922, she lost all her money. Among other things, she would no longer be able to pay for Muriel's education at Smith College.

Now the Earharts took in boarders to try to make ends meet. One of them was Sam Chapman, a tall, handsome chemistry engineer from Massachusetts with blue eyes and dark hair. He fell in love with Amelia.

Many of Amelia's friends were men, and she had dated many men. But Sam was different. For the first time in her life, she seemed to be in love. Her family were sure they would get married sooner or later.

Amelia took Sam seriously because he took *her* seriously, and he admired her courage and spirit. They both liked to swim and play tennis and discuss books. More important, they were both idealistic, concerned about problems such as fair wages for laborers.

Amelia felt guilty about her parents' money troubles, because they had invested in the mine on her advice. She couldn't give up her passion for flying, but she could try to earn a decent living. She took photographs, sold sausages, and even drove a gravel truck, to the horror of some of her friends. Meanwhile, in October 1922 she set a new altitude record for women, with her astonished father and sister watching from the stands.

But Amy and Edwin Earhart's marriage fell apart beyond repair. In 1923, Amy and the girls moved out to Sunset Boulevard in

Hollywood. Luckily this home was only a short drive from the new Glendale airport. At the airport's opening in March 1923, Amelia was a featured attraction in "The Ladies Sportplane Special." That May, Amelia took the test to get her official pilot's license. This test included a "dead stick" landing, in which she had to turn off the engine at almost five thousand feet in the air, glide down to the runway, and land within a certain distance of a set point.

In 1924, Edwin Earhart divorced his wife of twenty-nine years, and there was nothing more that their daughters could do to keep them together. Now Muriel wanted to return to Massachusetts and finish her college degree, and Amy decided to leave California and live with her in the Boston area. Amelia, too, made plans to return to the East Coast and go back to school.

At Home at Denison House

Amelia had been planning for some time to fly across the country. But by the summer of 1924, she was suffering from her old problem, a sinus infection. The pressure in her head, which was worse at high altitudes, made it painful to fly. She sold her plane, a new Kinner Airster, and had surgery to drain the infection.

Anyone else would have then taken the train to the East Coast, as Muriel had already done. Instead, Amelia bought a bright yellow Kissel, a touring automobile. She was worried about her mother, and she hoped that the adventures of a long trip would help take Amy's mind off the divorce.

So in June, Amelia and Amy set off on a roundabout route across the continent. They visited Sequoia National Park in northern California, Crater Lake in Oregon, Lake Louise and Banff in Canada, and Yellowstone in Wyoming. In some parts of the country the roads were "awful," as Amelia wrote her trucking partner, Lloyd Royer. Cheerfully she added, "We have had only one hint of trouble with the motor—the head gasket blew out."

Amelia's surgery in California had not really cured her sinus infection, though. By the time they reached Boston, she was suffering from it again. She had to be hospitalized and have more surgery. The pain was bad, but even worse for Amelia was waiting most of that fall to recover. She lived with her sister and mother in Medford, where Muriel had found a teaching job.

That winter Amelia went back to school at Columbia University in New York City. She was still not completely well, but by January 1925 she had perked up enough to climb on the dome of the library again. In March she registered at Columbia to take a degree in engineering.

Now Amelia's main problem was that she had no money. She could barely scrape together the fifty-six dollars to register for two college courses. She was counting on receiving a good amount of money when her partner in California sold their gravel truck, but the truck didn't bring that much. Also, she felt her partner needed the money even more than she did, and she insisted on splitting it with him.

Amelia had a good friend in New York, Marian Stabler, who could have lent her money. But Amelia was too proud to borrow money from a friend or even to admit how poor she was. Another reasonable solution would have been for Amelia to sell her Kissel car, her one expensive possession. But now that she didn't own an airplane, it was the jaunty yellow touring car that let her feel free and independent. She couldn't bear to part with it.

In April, completely out of money, Amelia gave up the struggle and dropped out of Columbia. Driving her Kissel car north to Boston, she moved back in with her sister and mother. She applied to the Massachusetts Institute of Technology for a scholarship in engineering, but she was turned down because she was female.

This was a low point for Amelia. She was twenty-eight, and she had no money. Worst of all, for such an idealistic person, she had no clear goal for her life.

Sam Chapman, now an engineer for

Boston Edison, wanted her to marry him. But marriage was not Amelia's idea of an answer to the question of what to do with her life. She continued to see Sam, sometimes with Muriel and her boyfriend, Albert Morrissey. Her friend Louise Schweinitz was now an intern at a Boston hospital, and Amelia often drove her and her husband to Marblehead Neck for beach parties with Sam. Sometimes on weekends Amelia went to airfields, just to be around planes and pilots. But she couldn't afford to fly, let alone buy a plane of her own.

Amelia worked at various jobs, but nothing she was truly committed to. First she tutored blind students, then she taught English to immigrants, and then she worked for six months at a mental hospital as a nurse-companion. Finally, in August 1926, Amelia registered with the Women's Educational and Industrial Union in Boston. She didn't know exactly what kind of job she was looking for, but even so she impressed the interviewer. "Has pilot's license," the woman noted on the interview form.

The interviewer sent Amelia to Denison House, where they had an opening for a part-time social worker. Denison, in Boston's South End, was one of the first settlement houses. These community centers in poor neighborhoods provided immigrants with medical care, recreation, classes in English, and other services they badly needed. Marion Perkins, the director of Denison House, was also impressed with Amelia, and she put her in charge of adult education. Then, seeing that Amelia had a special way with young people, she had her run the girls' program.

Amelia fit right into the spirit of Denison House. This was not a charity to patronize immigrants, but to help them help themselves. The immigrants she worked with—mainly Syrian and Chinese—loved her. She

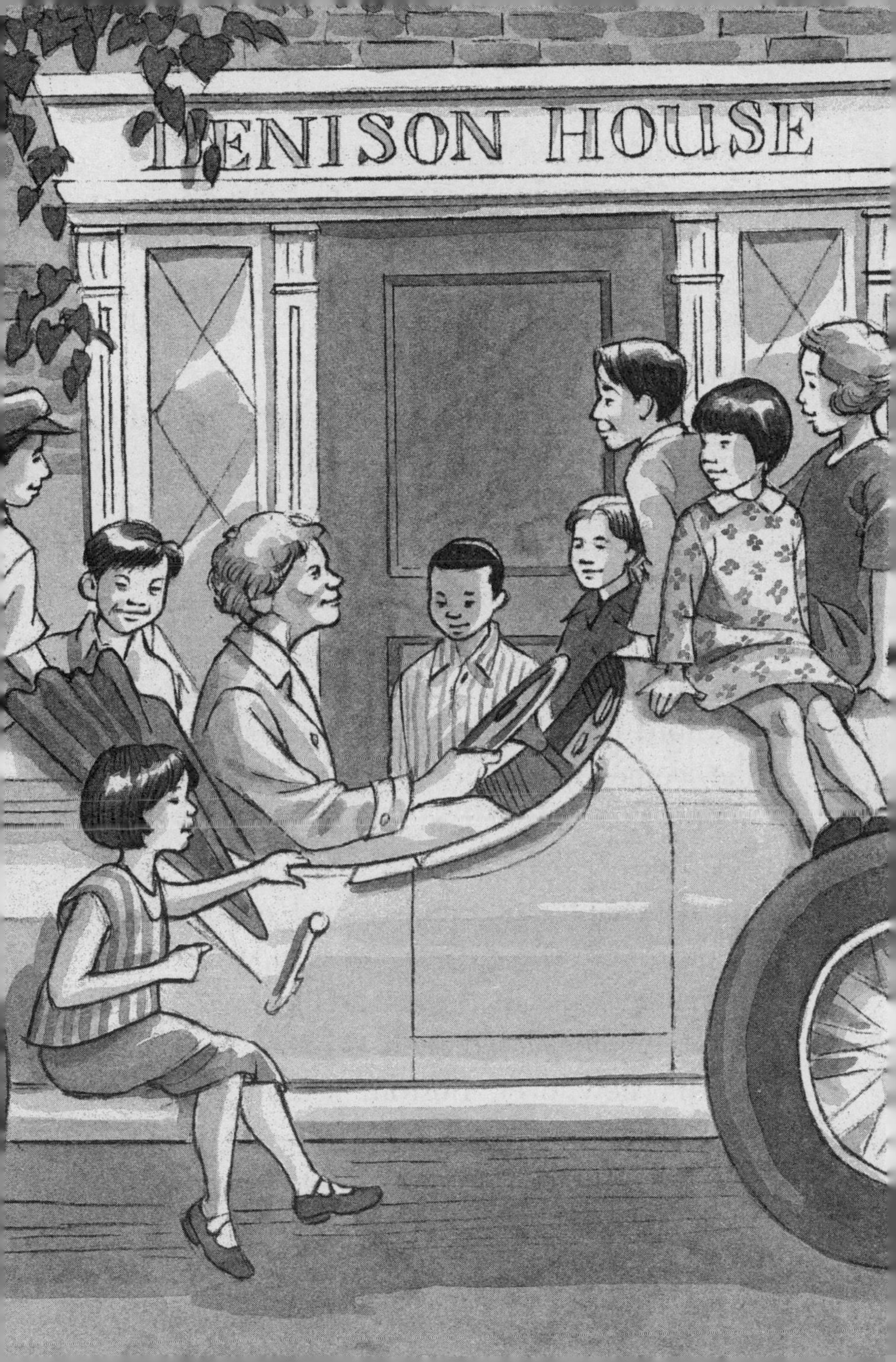
DENISON HOUSE

had a natural verve for organizing basketball teams, girls' clubs, and home classes for mothers. She delighted sick children, and their parents, by driving them to Massachusetts General Hospital in her yellow touring car.

Social work drew out Amelia's gifts for leading and encouraging other people. Also, after her hard times as a teenager, she had a natural sympathy for struggling families. Believing that having fun was as important as learning English, she often drove a carful of girls from the inner city to the Earharts' house in Medford for a picnic or marshmallow roast. She seemed to have found her calling at last.

Now that Amelia had a regular salary, she was able to fly sometimes. She joined the Boston chapter of the National Aeronautic Association. In May 1927, Amelia performed a publicity stunt for Denison House.

In a plane piloted by a Harvard student, Amelia flew over Boston, scattering free passes to a carnival to benefit the settlement house. The Boston papers reported the stunt, printing photos of "female pilot" Amelia in flying clothes. It was good publicity for Denison House, especially because these days there was great excitement about flying.

Only a few days earlier, former Air Mail Service pilot Charles Lindbergh had given an enormous boost to aviation. He was the first person to fly nonstop across the North Atlantic Ocean, landing in France on May 21. Overnight, he became the most famous man in the world. He was welcomed as a hero in Europe, and then cheered by huge crowds when he returned to the United States. The public was wild for lanky, modest, boyish-looking Lindbergh and for aviation in general.

Ever since she left California, Amelia had kept in touch with Bert Kinner. Now he put her in touch with Harold Dennison (no connection with Denison House), who planned to open a new airfield near Boston. Dennison met Bert Kinner in Los Angeles, making arrangements to sell Kinner planes on the East Coast, and Bert advised him to look up Amelia. Dennison quickly realized that Amelia would be good publicity for his airfield, too. He invited her to join the board of directors of the business, as well as to demonstrate Kinner aircraft for customers.

Dennison Airport opened in Quincy, just south of Boston, in July 1927, shortly before Amelia's thirtieth birthday. A crowd of 2,500 turned out to see the air show, and a reporter from the *Boston Herald* interviewed Amelia. The reporter seemed to think that a flying woman was startling news, but Amelia said firmly, "I think any normal woman should be able to learn to fly."

Amelia saw that women needed encouragement and support in order to make their way in aviation. She started to think about organizing a group of professional women flyers, and she wrote to the well-known pilot

Ruth Nichols to see if she was interested. Amelia also began to realize that she could use her growing reputation to promote aviation, and women in aviation. She applied to Zonta, the first organization for business and professional women, as a director of Dennison Aircraft Corporation.

During a demonstration at Dennison Airport that December, a young German woman pilot was forced to make a crash landing in the nearby swamp. Amelia knew that the landing showed the pilot's good sense and skill, but she also knew that not many people would understand this. And the newspapers had a habit of jumping on any hint that women pilots were incompetent. To distract the crowd while the other pilot was pulled from the swamp, Amelia jumped into another plane and put on a dazzling flying demonstration. Afterward, she explained to a reporter that she was proving "that women are quite as capable pilots as men, and quite as daring."

Amelia was still engaged to Sam Chapman. But the more Sam pressed her about a wedding date, the less interested she seemed. He felt that she was too involved in her work, and he didn't want his wife to work outside the home at all.

In the fall of 1927, Amelia was promoted to full-time resident at Denison House. She moved into one of the red brick row houses on Tyler Street to live, and she was elected one of the directors. With a full salary, Amelia was financially independent. She felt that life was opening up to her again.

In 1927, the year after Charles Lindbergh's nonstop flight across the Atlantic, many others tried to follow him. Most of them failed, and some of them, including three women pilots, died in the attempt. But that didn't stop others from trying.

One of the pilots eager to become the first woman to fly across the Atlantic was Amy

Guest. Amy Guest was wealthy and adventurous, accustomed to flying and big game hunting. Getting her friend the explorer Richard Byrd to help her, she bought his powerful tri-motor Fokker and hired a pilot and a mechanic. The Fokker was not a seaplane, but she planned to have it fitted with pontoons instead of wheels. She intended to end her transatlantic flight with a dramatic gesture, landing the *Friendship* (as she named the plane) on the Thames River in London, in front of the Houses of Parliament.

But Amy Guest's family found out about her risky plans, and they begged her until she agreed not to attempt the flight herself. However, she was still determined that a woman should have the honor and glory of flying across the Atlantic Ocean. But not just any woman. This woman must have a noble spirit and a fine character, she should be educated and well bred, and she should be a pilot.

Around this time George P. Putnam, a publisher, happened to hear about the project. George was a genius at creating publicity for his authors, and he had already published several best-selling books about real-life adventures. His titles included Commander Richard Byrd's *Skyward*, about his flight over the North Pole; and Charles Lindbergh's *We*, about his historic transatlantic flight. Another of George's books, *Wings*, about the heroic fighter pilots of World War I, was being made into a film, and would win the first Academy Award for best picture.

George knew that a successful transatlantic flight by a woman would turn her into an instant celebrity, and turn any book she wrote into an instant best-seller. The question was, who was the right woman to fly on the *Friendship*? Through his contacts in Boston, George found out about Amelia Earhart.

Early in 1928, Amelia wrote an article,

"When Women Go Aloft," for the fashionable magazine *The Bostonian*. Amelia's purpose was to promote flying, but the result of the article was to promote Amelia Earhart, too. A drawing of Amelia in flying clothes appeared alongside the article. She confidently described women as "hopelessly adventurous," and she explained why she loved flying so much. There was the excitement, of course, but there was also "the beauty of adventure."

It was about the same time that Amelia wrote a poem expressing her passion for taking risks. "Courage is the price that life exacts for granting peace," it began. These were the words of a young woman who loved adventure.

One afternoon in April, Amelia got a call at Denison House. She was busy looking after various games and classes, and not very eager to take the call. But she changed her mind when the caller, an agent for Amy Guest, explained his business: Amelia had been recommended as someone who might be a fitting first woman to fly the Atlantic.

A few weeks later, George Putnam interviewed Amelia in New York. He was busy and kept her waiting at first, and then he didn't bother to be especially polite. She was only one of several women they were looking over. But as soon as they began talking, he realized that this tall, slender young woman with the direct gaze and quietly confident manner was looking *him* over, too. And he quickly became convinced that she was the ideal person for the flight.

When George asked Amelia why she wanted to fly the Atlantic, she smiled at him, a smile that said the answer was obvious. "Why does a man ride a horse?" she asked him in turn.

George had to smile back. He was very much at home on a horse himself. And what made him the happiest, besides going after a big business deal, was being out in the wilderness on an adventure. "Because he wants to, I guess," he answered.

"Well then." Amelia laughed, and so did George.

The Beauty of Adventure

Within a few days, Amelia was informed that she had the job, if she wanted it. There would be no pay, except for her expenses. Bill Stultz, an experienced pilot and navigator, would fly the *Friendship*, although Amelia would have a chance to take the controls if the weather was clear.

Amelia did want this adventure, very much.

Now George took charge of the publicity,

which would be important for the success of the book he wanted Amelia to write. The record-breaking flight must create a sensation, but not too soon. So preparations for the flight were made in secret, to avoid being overrun with reporters and interviewers and photographers. The *Friendship* was being outfitted at a hangar near Boston, and the press knew that. But they assumed it was still Commander Byrd's plane, destined to fly him across the South Pole.

At the same time, George was planning for an enormous wave of publicity, once the flight was under way. He sold the newsreel rights to the story to Paramount News. He had Amelia pose for photographs, wearing flight helmet and jacket, on the roof of the Copley Plaza Hotel. The photographer deliberately played up Amelia's resemblance to Charles Lindbergh—both were tall and slim, with short fair hair and a modest, straightforward manner.

As Amelia got to know George, she was impressed with his intelligence. He could be rude and overbearing, but he could also be very charming, and he turned on his charm for Amelia. She was fascinated with the way this man pursued business deals, sometimes several at once, like a predator stalking its prey.

"Do you know who you remind me of?" Amelia asked George one day. "You're Simpkin, the cat in Beatrix Potter's *The Tailor of Gloucester*. He liked to have several projects going at once, so he kept extra mice under upside-down teacups."

Visiting the hangar at a field north of Boston, Amelia caught her first glimpse of the aircraft that was supposed to carry her over eighteen hundred miles of empty ocean. Its body was red-orange, its wings gold colored. "It'll show up well if we have to land in the water," thought Amelia.

The *Friendship* was a Fokker, a Dutch-made plane, with a wingspan of seventy-two feet. With its three strong motors, it could fly as fast as 129 miles per hour. It was sturdy enough to carry almost nine hundred gallons of fuel, extremely important for the long non-stop flight. Amelia was impressed with the instrument panel: altimeter, gas gauge, speedometer, compasses, wind drift instruments, and even a radio for communication with the ground and ships.

Amelia was also impressed with Bill Stultz and Lou Gordon, the pilot and mechanic of the *Friendship*. Bill was an experienced flyer, he was familiar with the Fokker, and he would have been Commander Byrd's first choice for his expedition to Antarctica. Also, he was experienced in flying "blind" through fog and clouds, by reading the instruments rather than looking out the window. Amelia had no training in instrument flying, and they agreed that she would take the controls only if the weather was clear.

Because she was well known around

Boston, Amelia had to stay away from the hangar most of the time. She kept her plans secret, although she told her employers—Marion Perkins at Denison House and Harold Dennison of Dennison Aircraft Corporation—and her fiancé, Sam Chapman. But she did not tell her mother or sister. She took a two-week leave from Denison House, expecting to return to her social work after the flight—if she survived.

In case Amelia was killed during the flight, she left letters to be sent to her mother and father—"popping off" letters, she cheerfully called them. "Hooray for the last grand adventure!" she wrote her father. "I wish I had won, but it was worthwhile, anyway."

Just before she left Boston, Amelia mailed a letter to Muriel, explaining what she was doing and why it had to be kept secret. "I didn't want to worry Mother, and she would suspect if I told you. . . . Please explain all to Mother. I couldn't stand the added strain of telling Mother and you personally."

Amelia didn't have much packing to do, because she would take only the clothes she was wearing: brown riding pants and boots, a white silk shirt, a red necktie, a brown sweater, her leather jacket, and two silk scarves. She also had a fur-lined flying suit. She packed a small knapsack with toothbrush and comb, two handkerchiefs, a camera, binoculars, and a leather-bound diary that George Putnam had given her to take notes in. George had sold exclusive rights to her story to the *New York Times*, so she had to keep a careful record of the flight and write it up quickly afterward.

Amelia and her crew decided to fly the *Friendship* northeast from Boston to Newfoundland, and then to refuel for the flight across the Atlantic. That plan would cut several hundred miles off the nonstop route from North America to England.

First, the crew had to wait three days for the right weather conditions to take off from Boston Harbor. They were receiving the latest weather news from Dr. James Kimball of the weather bureau in New York, so that they knew the forecast for England as well as northeastern North America.

The third day was clear, and Amelia and her crew decided to try for it. After four attempts, and leaving behind thirty gallons of fuel as well as the backup pilot, the *Friendship* managed to lift off. But they only got as far as Nova Scotia before fog closed in, and they had to land in Halifax.

The next morning the *Friendship* flew from Halifax to Trepassey, a small fishing village in Newfoundland. This would be their takeoff point for the transatlantic flight. But here the weather forced them to wait again, this time for a week and a half.

There was no keeping the flight secret anymore, and Amelia's name appeared in headlines across the country. Angry that the press seemed to think she was going to make a lot of money from the flight, Amelia telegraphed to George Putnam: "PLEASE GET THE POINT ACROSS THAT THE ONLY STAKE I WIN IS THE PRIVILEGE OF FLYING AND THE PLEASURE OF HAVING SHARED IN A FINE ADVENTURE WELL CONDUCTED WHOSE SUCCESS WILL BE A REAL DEVELOPMENT AND PERHAPS SOMETHING OF AN INSPIRATION FOR WOMEN."

The delay was caused partly by fog and partly by Trepassey Harbor, which was narrow. The *Friendship* could take off in only one direction, southwest, and only if the wind was from the right direction to lift the nose of the plane. Supposedly the *Friendship*'s pontoons made the plane safer in a flight across the ocean, since it could land on water. But they also added to the weight and slowed the plane down on takeoff, especially if the waves were rough. The problem was, could the *Friendship* carry enough fuel to fly across the

Atlantic, and still be light enough to take off under difficult conditions?

To add to the strain, Amelia and her pilot and copilot knew they were in a race with two other women poised to cross the Atlantic. One, Mabel Boll, was flying a faster plane, the *Columbia*. Another, Thea Rasche, was a German aviator who planned to fly across the Atlantic from Newfoundland to Berlin, Germany.

"None of us are sleeping much anymore," Amelia wrote in her log. ". . . We are on the ragged edge." Bill Stultz relieved the tension of waiting by drinking heavily. Amelia wondered if she should ask George to send a replacement pilot.

Still, Amelia managed to keep her sense of humor. George's telegrams helped. To pass the time, he suggested, Amelia could write an outline of her story of the flight, to be filled in later when she arrived in England. As for her complaints about having to wear the same clothes for a week and a half: "THINK OF FRESH WARDROBE IN LONDON AND GRIN." He signed the telegram, with a slight misspelling: "SIMKIN."

On Sunday, June 17, 1928, the weather at Trepassey was finally favorable for takeoff. Bill Stultz was suffering from heavy drinking the night before, and he was worried about the forecast for bad weather over the Atlantic. But Amelia, who had the final say, was more worried about Mabel Boll in the *Columbia* beating them.

Twice the *Friendship* tried to take off but failed to reach fifty miles per hour, the minimum liftoff speed. In desperation, the crew unloaded two hundred gallons of their precious gasoline. On the third try, the *Friendship* staggered at last from the water, outboard engines sputtering. It circled the harbor and disappeared into the northeast sky.

Two weeks after leaving Boston, Amelia was on her way across the Atlantic at last. But over the open ocean, they met towering thunderstorm clouds. The *Friendship* couldn't rise above them, because it was too heavy. They had to plow straight through the storm, with the plane shaking and rocking—the worst weather Amelia had ever flown through. And flying against the wind slowed them down further and used more fuel.

The pilot and copilot, in the cockpit, were warmed by the heat of the engines, but back in the cabin it was cold. Amelia wore earplugs against the deafening roar of the engines. There were no seats or even cushions, so she had to crouch on the pile of flying suits, between the gas tanks, or kneel at the window beside the chart table. Luckily she was very limber—Marian Stabler had noticed a few years earlier that Amelia could balance on her hands, with her knees tucked up to her chest, or sleep for hours curled up on one sofa cushion.

Amelia wrote in her logbook, her scrawling

handwriting made worse by the jostling of the plane. She kept an anxious eye on Bill Stultz, hoping he could keep up his concentration through the hours ahead. She was dismayed to find a bottle of liquor in Bill's gear, and she wondered if she should drop it through the trapdoor. But he now seemed alert and steady, and he did not come back looking for his bottle.

As the night went on and the fuel tanks emptied, the plane grew lighter. They were able to rise through the gigantic columns of cumulus clouds and finally, at ten thousand feet, above the clouds. It was calmer up here, but so cold that all three of them put on their fur-lined flying suits. Amelia wrote in her logbook (mostly about clouds), and took pictures out the one small window. At one point she slept briefly.

Amelia and Bill and Lou were grateful to see the first faint streaks of dawn ahead of them. But now the crew of the *Friendship* were not sure where they were. The clouds were patchy, and the pilot brought the plane down lower, but all they could see was water. The radio seemed to be dead, and the air speed indicator and wind drift indicators were not precise enough to be very helpful.

"Port motor coughing," wrote Amelia in her logbook. Fuel was running low. If they were not near land, they were in trouble.

They crossed the paths of several ships, and finally they decided to try dropping a note onto a steamer below. Although they couldn't send a radio message to the ship, they might be able to receive a message. Or maybe the ship could paint its position on the deck so they could see it from the air. Amelia tied a note, asking for the position, to an orange and aimed it out the window. It missed the deck and disappeared under the waves. They considered landing near the ship, where at least they had a chance of rescue.

But that would mean the failure of their

mission. Amelia and her crew decided to fly on. But they were afraid they would run out of fuel if they tried to make England, as they'd hoped, so they planned to land in Ireland.

For another tense hour and a half the three on the *Friendship* waited to sight land. Then the solid dark edge of a coastline finally appeared through the mist. With a whoop of excitement, Slim threw a half-eaten sandwich out the window.

By now there was so little gasoline left that the engines worked only when the plane was flying level. Gratefully they glided down through the rain onto the gray surface of a large bay. As it turned out, they had flown south of the tip of Ireland and landed at the little seacoast town of Burry Port, Wales. Amelia Earhart was the first woman to fly nonstop from North America to Europe.

Amelia had spent a tense day and night without any real rest. But while the pilot was arranging to refuel the plane, she dutifully wrote the first installment of the story she had promised the *New York Times* and the *London Times*.

By the time Amelia set foot on solid ground at Burry Port, a crowd of thousands had gathered. Suddenly, to her amazement, she was famous. Policemen held back the cheering throng, but even so, some souvenir-seeker grabbed the silk scarf from Amelia's head.

The next day, the *Friendship* flew on to Southampton, England, where even larger crowds greeted the heroes. Meanwhile, back in the United States, George Putnam was not at all amazed by Amelia's fame. He made sure that the story of her flight appeared on front pages throughout the world.

President Coolidge telegraphed Amelia his congratulations. She telegraphed back: "SUCCESS ENTIRELY DUE GREAT SKILL OF MR. STULTZ." The pilot was only 1 mile off course,

she explained, after flying "blind" for 2,246 miles.

In the following weeks, Amelia repeated over and over that the glory should go to Bill Stultz and Slim Gordon, but no one paid any attention. The press picked up the nickname "Lady Lindy," playing on her resemblance to the hero Charles Lindbergh. All the headlines were about the amazing "Woman's Triumph."

In London, Amelia was the center of one party and reception after another. Amy Guest, overjoyed with the success of her plan and with Amelia herself, invited her to stay at her house. She lent her clothes, since Amelia had only riding breeches and a leather jacket. The Prince of Wales, who loved to fly himself, danced with Amelia at one of the parties. At a public luncheon, Amelia sat between Winston Churchill and Lady Astor, and she spoke to the audience on the future of aviation.

Amelia remained poised and gracious in

such famous company and with so much attention. But she managed to sneak away one day to fly at a nearby airport. Lady Mary Heath, an English pilot who had flown solo from England to South Africa and back, had invited Amelia to try out her plane, an Avro Avian. Amelia did—and loved it so much that she decided to buy it.

Another day Amelia spent in London's West End, visiting the settlement house that had inspired Denison House in Boston. In the midst of all the busyness, she was glad to get a letter from George Putnam. She answered him with a telegram: "THANKS CHEERING LETTER . . . SIMPKIN SWELL GUY."

After two weeks of celebrity, Amelia was relieved to board the S.S. *President Roosevelt* and sail back to the United States. She finally had some time to herself, to think about what the flight of the *Friendship* meant. This immense lonely expanse of ocean that she had crossed, west to east, ten days before—

she and the *Friendship* might easily have disappeared beneath these waves forever.

Back in New York, the whole city celebrated. Amelia and Bill Stultz and Slim Gordon were paraded up Broadway, Mayor Jimmy Walker handed them keys to the city, and Commander Richard Byrd hosted a luncheon in their honor. "GIRL FLIER, SHY AND SMILING, SHARES PRAISE WITH MATES," ran a headline in the *New York Times*. Thirty-two U.S. cities wanted to celebrate Amelia like this, George Putnam informed her.

Amelia thought that Boston, Chicago, and Pittsburgh would be quite enough. Even after all the celebrations, after being treated like royalty, after the flood of telegrams and letters, Amelia still didn't quite understand that her life was changed forever. She kept telling reporters that she was merely on leave from Denison House.

Boston was next. Here she was welcomed at the airport by Amy and Muriel Earhart—

and more than 250,000 other people. In the following hectic days of more parties and receptions, she managed to slip away to Medford for a brief visit with her mother and sister. Sam Chapman took her to Marblehead for a few private hours.

Amelia also fit in a visit to Denison House, where she chatted with the children and their families, just as if she were not a world-famous heroine. But by now Amelia was beginning to realize that she would not, after all, be going back to social work.

In Chicago, Amelia especially enjoyed her visit to Hyde Park High School, where she had spent such a miserable, lonely year. She spoke cheerfully to the school assembly and then stepped from the stage onto the piano. This was the high-spirited Amelia who had been missing during the school year of 1914–1915.

By the time Amelia finished her lecture tour, she was good friends with both George

Putnam and his wife, the socialite Dorothy Binney Putnam. They invited her to Rye, New York, to work uninterrupted on the book she'd promised George. There was plenty of room in the Putnams' rambling sixteen-room house, set off by gardens and protected by oak and elm trees.

Amelia took breaks from writing for horse-back riding, swimming in Long Island Sound, parties, and evenings in nearby New York City. Still, George kept her to a strict schedule. She finished the book in two weeks and dedicated it to her hostess. George titled it *20 Hours 40 Minutes, Our Flight in the Friendship*, and he rushed it into print.

McCall's magazine invited Amelia to write for them, too. But they changed their minds when her name and picture appeared in an advertisement for Lucky Strike cigarettes— smoking was considered unladylike. Amelia was outraged by what she thought was inter-ference with her private life. She didn't smoke, and she didn't do the ad to get money for herself. She gave her share to Commander Byrd, in thanks for his help with the *Friendship* flight, for his new expedition to Antarctica.

In November 1928, during a trip to Boston, Amelia told Sam Chapman that she would not marry him, after all.

An Inspiration for Women

After the success of the *Friendship* flight, everyone wanted to hear Amelia Earhart speak and to read what she wrote. Invitations for her to lecture poured in, and the articles she wrote about flying were widely reprinted. *McCall's* might think Amelia Earhart wasn't ladylike enough for its readers, but the fashionable magazine *Cosmopolitan* was glad to hire her. They made her editor for the most exciting topic of the times—aviation. Amelia could also count on good royalties from *20 Hours 40 Minutes*, published in September 1928.

For the first time in her life, Amelia had plenty of money. She wrote her mother: "Please throw away rags and get things you need on my account at Filene's. I'll instruct them. I can do it now and the pleasure is mine."

It was also a pleasure for Amelia to be an honored guest at dedication ceremonies and parties with other celebrities. More important, she was delighted to see that she could actually make a career out of flying. As a famous person, she would be able to raise money for new adventures.

But it disturbed Amelia that she had not really done anything to deserve fame. Over and over again, she pointed out in interviews, speeches, and writing that she had only been a passenger on the *Friendship*. She longed to set a record as a *pilot*.

Amelia had her own plane now, the Avro Avian she had bought in England from Lady Mary Heath. The Avian was an open-cockpit biplane, small, light, and well built. At the end of August 1928 she brought it to Rye, New York, where she was still staying with George Putnam and his wife, Dorothy. Amelia kept the Avian on a polo field at the Westchester Country Club.

Amelia's new adventure, she decided, would be a flight across the country by herself. No woman pilot had done this before. It would be Amelia's first solo long-distance trip.

During the first half of September, Amelia flew to Pittsburgh, then over the Midwest in a series of hops, and on to the Southwest. At this time, one of the most difficult things about flying was simply finding the way. Aerial maps were so bad that flyers often used Rand McNally road maps, meant for automobile drivers. But there were not many signs that could be seen from the air.

"Imagine automobiling without signs!" Amelia wrote later in her story of her life, *The Fun of It*. "Imagine trying to recognize a new town the way flyers do—a hundred-mile-an-hour look at a checkerboard of streets and roofs, trees and fields . . ." She begged for "large white or chrome yellow letters painted on some flat roof," announcing the name of each town. "An arrow pointing the direction to the nearest landing field is also desirable," she added dryly.

On this trip across the country Amelia gained valuable experience in dead reckoning—navigating by calculating how far the airplane had traveled, and in which direction. She safety-pinned maps to her shirt, to keep them from wafting out of the open cockpit. In spite of this, a map escaped as she flew over the Southwest. She had to land on the main street of a small town in Texas to ask directions.

In Pecos, Texas, Amelia was delayed by

repairs to her engine. And on the final leg of the journey, as she landed in a field of tall grass in Los Angeles, her plane turned over completely. But none of these setbacks disturbed Amelia. She was purely happy to be back in the air, by herself. Minor problems were part of the great adventure of flying.

These adventures made fine articles for *Cosmopolitan*. Photographs of Amelia also appeared in the magazine, often wearing the slacks she found so practical for flying—and so flattering to her slender, long-legged figure. For the first time, pants became an acceptable fashion for women.

Amelia was also hired by Transcontinental Air Transport (which would become TWA), a new company offering trips across the country in an astounding forty-eight hours. Part of her job was designing airplane interiors and waiting rooms at airports to be comfortable and appealing to women. Another part was giving lectures and writing magazine articles to promote air travel for ordinary people. Most people were still afraid to fly.

At the beginning of July 1929, Bill Stultz, the pilot of the *Friendship*, crashed his airplane while flying drunk. He and his passengers were killed. Attending his funeral in Manhasset, Long Island, Amelia thought about that long night over the Atlantic Ocean. If Bill had decided to come back to the cabin for the bottle in his tool bag, she might not be here now.

Right after the funeral, Amelia went into New York City and took part in a radio broadcast. The purpose was to reassure passengers about the safety of commercial flying, as opposed to the reckless stunt flying Bill Stultz had been doing.

Ever since their first interview in the spring of 1928, Amelia had been spending a great deal of time with George Putnam. As her manager, George made business and travel arrangements for Amelia, and often traveled with her. He gave her all kinds of advice, from how to make speeches to what she should wear.

"Your hats!" wrote George, after seeing some pictures of her in newspapers. "They are a public menace. You should do something about them when you must wear them at all." In those days it was as unusual for a woman to appear in public without a hat as it was for her to appear wearing pants. But the bareheaded, windblown curls style suited Amelia, and she made it her own.

Brilliant in public relations, George realized that Amelia was the perfect female celebrity for the 1920s. She was attractive in a healthy, athletic way, casual but well mannered, daring but not at all unfeminine. She enjoyed public appearances, and audiences loved her.

George loved the same qualities that audiences loved in Amelia, and more. By this time he was not only Amelia's manager—he had become her best friend. He respected her intelligence, and he admired her independence. They both loved horseback riding, the outdoors in general, and books. They both believed in a life of challenges and risks.

In December 1929, George's wife, Dorothy, divorced him by mutual agreement. The next month George proposed to Amelia, and she turned him down. He must have been surprised—tall, lean, and good-looking, George was used to bowling people over with his charm.

At this point Amelia had no intention of marrying George, or anyone else. In June of that year her sister, Muriel, had married Albert Morrissey, and Amelia had been her maid of honor. When reporters pestered Amelia about when *she* was going to get married, she smiled one of her big smiles. "I would make a poor wife, running around the country as I am."

194

Again George Putnam asked Amelia to marry him, and again she turned him down. "I think I may not ever be able to see marriage except as a cage," she wrote a friend. From watching her own parents, she had the impression of marriage as an unhappy entanglement that kept women from having fulfilling careers.

And Amelia's own career was becoming more and more fulfilling. She was the first woman to make a transcontinental round-trip flight. In August 1929 she had competed in the first Women's Air Derby, a race from Santa Monica, California, to Cleveland, Ohio. Amelia bought a new airplane before this race, a fast, streamlined Lockheed Vega, and she finished third. She'd helped establish the Ninety-Nines, an organization of women pilots, and she'd become its first president.

Amelia was also happy with her new independent way of living. She shared it with her mother as much as she could, sometimes taking

Mrs. Earhart along on her business trips. Amy Earhart, now in her sixties, gamely flew on Transcontinental Air Transport planes with her daughter, and Amelia pointed her out to encourage other women to fly. When Amelia was not on a lecture tour, or flying here and there, her home was the New York clubhouse of the American Woman's Association on West Fifty-seventh Street. Nothing could have been further from the lives of most women, or from the domestic life that her sister, now Muriel Earhart Morrissey, was settling into.

Back in 1925, when Amy and Edwin Earhart divorced, Edwin had stayed in California. He had married again. Later, he became seriously ill, and Amelia visited him on her trips to the West Coast. She paid off his mortgage so that Edwin and his second wife, Helen, would have a house free and clear.

In September 1930, Amelia got a message that her father was dying. She rushed back to California and spent a last few days with him. "He asked about you and Pidge a lot," she wrote her mother. ". . . He was an aristocrat as he went—all the weaknesses gone with a little boy's brown puzzled eyes." In the end, it was as if Amelia had become the parent and her father, the child.

Flying back from California after her father's funeral, Amelia had an accident at the naval air station in Norfolk, Virginia. Her plane ground-looped and landed on its back. Amelia suffered scalp injuries, but she wore a turban over the bandages on her head and went on with her speaking schedule.

Still, maybe the combination of her accident and her father's death shook Amelia enough to change her mind about marrying George. George would not be a conventional husband like Sam Chapman or Albert Morrissey, who expected a wife to stay home and keep house for them. George was willing to take Amelia on her own terms.

But George Putnam was *not* willing to take no for an answer—he was used to talking other people into saying yes. That October, he asked Amelia once more if she would marry him. They were at the unromantic setting of the Lockheed Aircraft factory in Burbank, California, and Amelia was about to fly out. By this time she must have made up her mind. She merely patted him on the arm, said, "Okay," and climbed into her airplane.

That November, George and Amelia applied for a marriage license. Still, Amelia, so brave in other ways, was very much afraid of getting married. She didn't tell her family that she was engaged.

Amelia didn't trust her mother or sister to keep a secret about her private life. And this secret was about the most private, tender side of Amelia Earhart. Also, she didn't trust

Amy or Muriel to understand her fears. After all, Amy Earhart had spent most of her life trying to stay married. And Muriel, in spite of seeing their parents so unhappy, had just gotten married herself.

On February 7, 1931, the day of her wedding to George, Amelia was still having qualms. Just before the ceremony, she handed George a letter spelling out her terms. "A sad little letter," he called it. He understood how terrified she was that marriage would ruin her life and their love for each other.

"Please let us not interfere with the other's work or play, not let the world see our private joys or disagreements," Amelia begged in the letter. She needed independence, and she would need to be by herself from time to time. And if, after one year, the marriage didn't seem to be working, he must let her go. George agreed.

He had already agreed that the wedding

would be completely private. They were married at his mother's house in Noank, Connecticut, by Judge Arthur Anderson, a family friend. Amelia wore her favorite color, brown, in a simple suit and blouse. The only witnesses were George's mother, George's uncle, the judge's son, and "twin black cats," as George playfully described it.

Two days after the wedding, Amelia and George both went back to work. They saw nothing strange about that, because they both loved their work. Besides, their work was very much tied up with each other.

Always curious, always looking for new experiences, Amelia was now intrigued with a new kind of airplane, the Pitcairn autogiro. The maker was eager to have Amelia Earhart's name connected with his aircraft, and she had already tried one out in December. The autogiro, with its long, bright green body, reminded Amelia of a dragonfly.

It could move like a dragonfly, too. With a rotor and long, narrow blades like a windmill mounted on top of the body, it could hover in the air and come straight down to the ground, slowly. This new kind of aircraft didn't need a large airfield to land or take off, and Pitcairn hoped that soon everyone would be driving autogiros instead of automobiles.

In April 1931, Amelia set a new altitude record for the autogiro, taking it up to over 18,000 feet. George arranged for Beech-Nut, the chewing gum company, to buy an autogiro for Amelia to fly across the country. The trip, including an article by Amelia in *Cosmopolitan*, "Your Next Garage May House an Autogiro," would publicize Pitcairn's aircraft. With "Beech-Nut" painted on the side of the autogiro in huge letters, Beech-Nut would also receive publicity.

Amelia did fly the whole trip from Newark to Oakland, California, and back to Newark. But long before the end, she was fed up with the autogiro. It was much more difficult to control than an ordinary airplane, especially on takeoff and landing. At an air fair in Abilene, Texas, Amelia got caught in a sudden windstorm and had to land in a parking lot, smashing up the autogiro and several cars.

In September 1931, flying a new autogiro into the Michigan State Fair in Detroit, Amelia dropped twenty feet to land heavily. The plane ground-looped and was wrecked. George, watching in horror, saw the splintered rotors disappear in what he thought was a cloud of smoke. Dashing forward, he tripped over a guy wire and broke three ribs. But there was no fire after all, and Amelia walked out of the cloud of dust unhurt.

Almost worse than the accidents, from Amelia's point of view, was the fact that the autogiro was awkward and slow. Its top speed was eighty miles an hour, not much faster than an automobile. It used so much fuel that it could only take short hops of about two hours.

In between flying and lecture dates, Amelia settled into the house in Rye that she now shared with George Putnam. The house was full of mementos of George's many adventures, including bearskins and walrus tusks and even shrunken human heads. The walls of one bedroom were painted to look like a jungle, and another with tropical fish and seaweed.

Amelia wanted to add her touch to the house, too, since this was her first real home of her own. She worked in the gardens, and she gathered around her things that she cared about. She asked her mother to send her grandmother's music books, as well as some books of poetry saved from the Atchison house library. Amelia also brought home a small wooden box of her papers: school diplomas, letters, and poems.

* * *

Meanwhile, May 1932, the fifth anniversary of Charles Lindbergh's historic flight, was coming up next year. Everyone was wondering who would be the first *woman* to fly solo across the Atlantic.

Solo Across the Atlantic

In the spring of 1931, while Amelia was flying the autogiro and enjoying married life with George, there was a new race on. Who *would* be the first woman pilot to fly solo across the Atlantic? In June, Ruth Nichols, who held both the speed record and the altitude record for women, tried first. But she crashed at St. John's, New Brunswick, before she even set out over the Atlantic. The accident broke several vertebrae in her back, but she was determined to try again.

Other top women pilots, including Elinor Smith and Laura Ingalls, were also preparing for the race. Amelia knew this, and that fall she worked the information into a new book she was writing. Part of this book was about her childhood and her life before flying. She also described, in a reassuring way, what it was like to fly. She summarized the history of women in aviation, from nineteenth-century balloonists to aviation pioneers such as Harriet Quimby to the well-known women who flew now. Amelia knew all the current women pilots, including Anne Morrow Lindbergh (Charles Lindbergh's wife), Louise Thaden, Laura Ingalls, and Elinor Smith.

By early 1932, Amelia had also decided to try for the transatlantic solo. "Would you *mind* if I flew the Atlantic?" she asked George at breakfast one morning. She didn't want to announce her intentions, as Elinor Smith and

Ruth Nichols had, because she wanted to be able to drop out quietly if she changed her mind. Without any publicity, she began to get ready.

Amelia hired the expert Norwegian pilot Bernt Balchen, an old friend of George's, as her aviation advisor. Working at the Teterboro, New Jersey, airport across the Hudson River, he would outfit her Lockheed Vega for the flight and help her plan the route and timing. Bernt also provided cover for Amelia, because he could pretend to reporters that he was preparing the plane for a South Pole expedition of his own. Most important, Amelia trusted him to advise her to give up the attempt, if he thought it was too dangerous.

The Lockheed Vega was the fastest and most reliable airplane of the time, but Amelia had been flying hers for almost three years. Bernt removed the old Wasp engine and replaced it with a new supercharged Wasp engine. Also, the plane needed special outfitting for a nonstop flight of more than two thousand miles. Bernt greatly increased the distance that Amelia's plane could fly by adding extra fuel tanks, boosting its gasoline capacity from 100 gallons to 420 gallons.

To improve the navigation, the Norwegian pilot added several new instruments. He tested the reconditioned plane over and over for safety. For her part, Amelia practiced flying "blind," with instruments only, in case the weather over the Atlantic kept her from navigating by the stars or landmarks.

During the spring of 1932, Amelia and George kept a close eye on the weather and the calendar. Doc Kimball, of the New York U.S. Weather Bureau, gave them daily weather bulletins, as he had for the flight of the *Friendship*. For maximum publicity, Amelia wanted to take off on May 20, five years exactly from the day Charles Lindbergh took off on his solo flight to France. But it was impossible to know, until the day before, if the weather would cooperate.

Meanwhile, Amelia wrote chatty letters to Amy Earhart in Massachusetts. "Have I ever sent you pix of the house? Now that spring is coming, I'd like you to see it as the garden grows." As before, she didn't tell her mother or sister about her plans.

Lucy Challis, Amelia's cousin and childhood friend, was staying in Rye with Amelia and George that spring. She was one of the few people Amelia let in on her secret, and she was surprised at how calm and relaxed Amelia seemed. She kept up her usual schedule of speaking engagements, gardened on weekends, and mingled with the guests who were always coming and going in the Putnam house.

On the morning of May 19, Amelia drove to the Teterboro airport for a routine practice flight. But George called from Doc Kimball's office in New York with the latest weather information: it looked good for the next day or so, but it would not hold. Now was the time to go.

Amelia jumped into her car and drove back to the house in Rye. It was a sunny spring day and the pink and white dogwoods were in full bloom, but she only glanced at the flowering garden. She grabbed her flying clothes, toothbrush, comb, a thermos and a can of tomato juice, and some charts, and sped back across the Hudson River to the airport. Twenty minutes later, she and Bernt Balchen and Eddie Gorski, the mechanic, took off for Harbor Grace, Newfoundland.

The next day, May 20, the weather held— not ideal, but good enough. Amelia took a long nap that afternoon, to be well rested if she made the attempt. She would take off at the end of the day and fly the Atlantic overnight, in order to take off and land in daylight.

That evening at the Harbor Grace airport,

Amelia consulted with Bernt Balchen one more time. "Do you think I can make it?" she asked with a direct look from her gray eyes. "You bet," he answered with a grin.

So at 7:20 Amelia shook hands with Bernt and her mechanic, climbed into the cockpit, and taxied down the rock and gravel runway. Although the plane was heavily laden with fuel for the long flight, Amelia took off smoothly into clear sunset skies.

The moon came up, and Amelia leveled off at twelve thousand feet. She was all by herself. The sky was above, the ocean below, and she was perfectly happy.

But after a few hours of flying, the altimeter failed. This had never happened to Amelia before in all her twelve years of flying. And it was serious, because the altimeter tells the pilot how high above the ground she is. When clouds or fog block the view, the altimeter can make the difference between life and death. For the moment, though, the sky was clear, and Amelia could judge the height of the plane by looking out the window.

Some time later, Amelia noticed flames flickering from a broken weld in the manifold ring. At this point she thought about turning back. But it was safer to fly on, she decided, than to try to land in the dark with a heavy load of fuel.

Farther on over the Atlantic, Amelia ran into a storm that was supposed to be south of her route. She couldn't fly over it or around it, so she plunged on through the lightning and the buffeting winds. In the turbulence, she went somewhat off course.

Later, Amelia tried to fly above the clouds to get her bearings from the stars. As she rose, she noticed ice on the windshield, and the engines labored—and then the Vega plunged into a spin. Amelia brought her plane out of the spin as the ice melted, close enough to the ocean for her to see the white-caps.

For some time Amelia flew below the clouds. Then fog closed in, and she decided it was too dangerous to fly low without an altimeter, and without being able to see the surface. Amelia never admitted it, but maybe at this point she wondered if she had been foolhardy to try the Atlantic crossing. The famous English pilot Lady Mary Heath had proclaimed in public that a woman could not fly the Atlantic alone—that it was suicide to try. Maybe Doc Kimball, who had also warned against it, was right. Maybe Amelia would never see her garden in Rye, or her mother and sister, or George, ever again.

Finally the Vega broke through to the dawn, and Amelia was able to climb above the clouds. The sunlight reflected from the snow-white clouds was dazzling, so she tried to fly just under the clouds. She sipped tomato juice from a straw.

Meanwhile, another problem came up. Amelia felt something wet on her neck, and she realized that gasoline was leaking from a broken fuel gauge. If the fumes reached the flames in the broken manifold, they could explode.

Amelia had hoped to fly all the way to France, as Charles Lindbergh had in 1927. But the wind had turned against her, which meant she had to use more fuel to keep up the same speed. How long would the fuel last? Amelia was also concerned about the broken exhaust manifold, which was now vibrating badly. She suspected that she had gotten off course, flying through the storm.

Seeing land below, Amelia knew she must be on the far side of the Atlantic Ocean— probably somewhere over Ireland. She spotted railroad tracks and circled, looking for an airfield. She didn't find one, but she chose a long pasture instead, and the Vega swooped down to earth among the astonished cows.

The one human in sight, a farmworker, gaped at the person dressed in riding pants,

with rumpled, curly hair, climbing out of the plane. *Was it a man or a woman?* he wondered.

"Where am I?" Amelia called to him.

He found his voice and answered, "In Gallegher's pasture."

In fact, Amelia was on a farm outside of Londonderry, a city in Northern Ireland. She had eaten and drunk nothing during the flight except a can of tomato juice, and she had flown without any relief or rest for almost fifteen hours. But before she slept, bathed, or ate, she got a ride into Londonderry and made her reports to the newspapers.

Then she called George, who had spent the night pacing—he didn't have Amelia's talent for remaining calm. But now that his wife was safe on the ground, he could laugh at the way she described the last few hours of her flight. She had kept the plane low over the ocean, in case the leaking fumes did catch fire, because "I'd rather drown than burn."

By the next day, a crew from Paramount

News had showed up, as well as a crowd of reporters and photographers. Amelia was used to media attention now, and she was poised and cheerful as she answered questions and posed beside the Vega. For the newsreels, she put on her flying suit and reenacted her landing in the pasture, while a watching crowd cheered and tossed their hats in the air. Amelia had already received a pile of congratulatory telegrams, including ones from President Hoover, the prime minister of Britain, the Lindberghs, and Governor and Eleanor Roosevelt.

Then Amelia was flown to London by Paramount, which had again bought exclusive rights to filmed interviews with her. She was now the most famous woman in the world, but she joked modestly in interviews about her record-breaking achievement. "When there is a traffic jam on Fifth Avenue men always comment, 'Oh, it's a woman driving.' So I determined to show them."

217

Amelia also joked that she had brought only twenty dollars with her, and no change of clothes. Naturally Selfridge's department store in London was delighted to furnish the American aviator with a wardrobe. They also shipped the Vega from Ireland to London, and displayed it to curious crowds in their store.

Amelia gave speech after speech and attended parties and receptions. The Prince of Wales invited her to St. James Palace. In spare moments she wrote the final chapter, "Across the Atlantic—Solo," of her new book, titled *The Fun of It*. She cabled it to her publishers in New York, so they could bring the book out immediately and get the most from the publicity.

Meanwhile, George crossed the Atlantic in the ordinary way, by ship, and joined Amelia in France. She had hoped to land there, and they had prepared great celebrations for her. In Paris, Amelia was awarded the Cross of the Knight of the Legion of Honor, the same medal that Charles Lindbergh had received. Then Amelia and George visited Rome and Brussels for more celebrations and more honors.

Finally, almost a month after her landing in Ireland, Amelia and George sailed for New York on the *Ile de France*. As the ocean liner left the harbor, three French airplanes escorted it and showered the deck with flowers. Fortunately the ocean voyage gave Amelia a chance to rest, because back in the United States, even more attention and honors were showered upon her. At a grand ceremony in Constitution Hall, she was awarded a gold medal by the National Geographic Society. President Herbert Hoover personally presented the medal to her.

In her acceptance speech, Amelia hoped that her flight had done something for women in aviation. "If it has," she said, "I shall feel it was justified."

In fact, her flight had done more than that. It showed how far airplanes had come since Charles Lindbergh's flight five years ago, and it reassured people that flying was safe. It encouraged manufacturers to invest in improving airplanes.

After a ticker-tape parade down Broadway in New York, and the celebrations in Washington, Amelia went on to a triumphal reception in Boston on June 29. Her mother and sister came to the airport to meet her, but they were even further in the background than after the *Friendship* flight. Amy and Muriel watched Amelia pose for pictures, head a procession from the airport to her hotel, greet VIPs, and take the place of guest of honor at a banquet.

The next morning, Amelia flew George to Los Angeles. "It was nice seeing you even in the rush," she wrote her mother from Los Angeles. She enclosed a check for one hundred dollars.

Many more cities were eager to welcome Amelia Earhart, and George arranged a tight-packed speaking schedule for the fall. But Amelia was not one to take it easy and ride on her last achievement, even for a short while. She had already decided on a new challenge: She would become the first woman to fly nonstop across the United States.

On July 10, less than two months after her solo transatlantic flight, Amelia took off from Los Angeles. But she was not able to complete a nonstop flight. A faulty fuel line forced her to stop in Columbus, Ohio, before flying on to Newark, New Jersey. She returned to Los Angeles for the beginning of the Olympic Games, at which U.S. Vice President Curtis awarded her the Distinguished Service Cross.

But Amelia had not given up her new challenge, and on August 24 she took off from the Los Angeles airport again. She brought along her usual skimpy provisions: hard-boiled eggs, a thermos of cocoa made by her cousin Lucy, and a can of tomato juice. The next morning she landed in Newark.

"Perfect flight, no stops!" she shouted as she climbed out of the "little red bus," her nickname for the Lockheed Vega. Her blond curls were blown by the breeze, and there was a big grin on her face. She was the first woman to span the continent nonstop, and she had set a record for nonstop distance flying for women. And she looked the part of a modern heroine, a slim, tall woman in tan riding pants and a short-sleeved tan silk shirt, topped with a jaunty bronze and yellow silk scarf.

Amelia and George's life was more hectic than ever. He was now working with Paramount Studios, which meant that he had to spend much of his time in Los Angeles. But hectic seemed to be the way they both liked it. And when they were together, they took time for silliness as well as grand plans.

A friend remembered them out in their yard at Rye, George pushing Amelia around the lawn in a wheelbarrow. George glared with mock determination, while Amelia laughed and shrieked. She might be a world-famous celebrity, but she could be as carefree as the girl who once careened down her homemade roller coaster.

The Last Flight

Eleanor Roosevelt had telegraphed congratulations to Amelia after her triumphant landing in Ireland, but the two women did not meet until that November, 1932. Governor Franklin D. Roosevelt had just been elected president. Amelia came to Poughkeepsie, New York, to give a talk on aviation. The First Lady-to-be introduced Amelia to the audience. "I hope to know Miss Earhart more and more," said Eleanor, "but I never hope to admire her more than I do now."

That was the beginning of a warm friendship.

Eleanor Roosevelt and Amelia Earhart had a natural understanding. They were both independent women who longed to do something worthwhile with their lives. They were both drawn to social work, and they both loved horseback riding. They had even both suffered from alcoholic fathers.

After Franklin's inauguration in 1933, Eleanor invited Amelia and George to the White House in April. Following the formal dinner that evening, Amelia took the First Lady for a ride in an Eastern Airlines plane. The two women were dressed in their long satin dresses and kid gloves, laughing at the adventure. Afterward, Eleanor wanted to take flying lessons herself, but her husband talked her out of it.

Amelia wrote her mother from the White House—not with descriptions of Washington high society, but with rather bossy advice. Amelia had sent Amy a couple of bottles of tooth wash, and she wanted to make sure she would use it. "My dentist says it is the best he knows." She also criticized the way her sister dressed her children in stockings and garters instead of the more up-to-date socks. "I'll buy em 6 pairs of sox each if she will use them."

Ever since her marriage to George in 1931, Amelia had been trying to persuade her mother to visit them in Rye. But Amy had not come, usually giving the reason that Muriel, with two children and no servants, needed her help in Medford. Maybe Amy was also resentful of George, who seemed to have taken over Amelia and swept her away into the life of the rich and famous. But in May 1933, Amy finally came to Rye.

Here she saw firsthand how Amelia lived now, on a quiet street sheltered by stately old trees. George and Amelia's house could comfortably hold two servants, a personal secretary, and a constant stream of guests: family, explorers, authors, Hollywood personalities, aviators. Besides gardens, the grounds included a croquet lawn and a lily pond, and the windows of the spacious sitting room overlooked a terrace.

That June, Amelia prepared to fly in the National Air Races, for the Bendix Trophy. Now in its third year, the most important race in the aviation world was finally open to women pilots. Amelia and Ruth Nichols were the only two women to enter.

Because of bad weather and mechanical problems, the race was a disaster. One pilot (male) was killed in a crash, and others had to drop out of the race. When the hatch cover of Amelia's plane blew open, she was forced to land in Arizona for repairs. She finished third, but she did not make good time.

Shortly after this race, a woman pilot, Florence Klingensmith, crashed to her death in another race. This accident was no different from the many accidents that male pilots had suffered, but it was used as an excuse to exclude women from the National Air Races. Such unfair discrimination only made Amelia more determined to encourage women to achieve. In her public appearances, she calmly stated, over and over, that women could pilot planes as well and as safely as men.

On her lecture tours, Amelia crisscrossed the country in her car. She would drive to a city and speak, then drive on to a lecture date in another city and speak again the next day, over and over, for weeks on end. Amelia encouraged women to go after careers in aviation. She knew it would not be easy, "but I feel that more will gain admittance as a greater number knock at the door. If and when you knock at the door, *it might be well to bring an ax along; you may have to chop your way through.*"

Shuttling back and forth across the country,

Amelia always took time to write letters to her mother. Once a month, she enclosed a check for the allowance she provided Amy. "The airline has taken a lot of time," she wrote in September 1933, "so much so that I have been unable to call Pidge, or see you, on my hasty visits to Boston . . ."

"The airline" was Boston-Maine Airways (later to become Northeast Airlines). It was founded by Paul Collins and Gene and Vidal, who had worked with Amelia at Transcontinental Air Transport. Collins was president, Vidal was a director. Amelia, vice president, worked on public relations and sales, especially encouraging women to fly. She drew big crowds, and ticket sales went up.

In another business venture, Amelia developed a line of comfortable, good-looking clothing for active women. She wore slacks most of the time now—tailored gabardine slacks in the daytime, elegant satin pajamas for evening wear. She liked shirts made of parachute silk, because it was strong, light, and washable.

Since George Putnam had to spend so much time in California with Paramount, in the fall of 1934 he and Amelia finally decided to rent a house there. They settled in the Toluca Lake section of North Hollywood, a short drive from the Lockheed factory in Burbank. Amelia's plane, a new Vega, was now being overhauled at Lockheed, because she was once again planning a record-setting adventure.

Amelia wanted to be the first person to fly solo over the Pacific Ocean between Hawaii and California. Seven pilots had already been killed on this route. The danger did not faze Amelia, but she saw no reason to take unnecessary risks. For one thing, she decided to begin her flight in Hawaii and end in California, rather than the other way around. "It's easier to hit a continent than an island," she explained in her offhand way.

To help her prepare for the flight, Amelia hired Paul Mantz. He was a gifted and experienced pilot and a neighbor of George and Amelia's in North Hollywood. His team of planes and pilots had done the stunt flying for the Academy Award-winning movie *Wings*, which had been George's idea.

Amelia's new Vega was a faster, more streamlined plane, with up-to-date equipment, including a two-way radiotelephone. The radio weighed eighty pounds, together with its generator, but it could be a lifesaver. She would be able to communicate with ships and coastal stations to confirm her position during flight—or to ask for rescue if she was forced down.

The fuel lines in Amelia's plane were covered with rubber, to prevent leaks like the one that occurred during her solo Atlantic flight. Extra fuel tanks were added so that the plane could hold 520 gallons. A backup altimeter was added, as well as other backup instruments.

Just before Christmas, Amelia and George and Paul Mantz and his wife sailed from Los Angeles for Hawaii. Amelia's plane was on board, too, strapped to the aft tennis deck of the ocean liner. From the ship, Amelia wrote her mother a long, chatty letter, enclosing some extra money. She added a few words of advice: "Reporters may call on you. If so, be pleasant, admit you're my mother if you care to, and simply say you're not discussing plans."

Once Amelia reached Hawaii and announced publicly that she was going to fly solo back to California, the newspapers showered her with criticism. It was only a month or so ago that the three-man crew of another plane, attempting an Oakland-to-Honolulu flight, had been lost at sea. The navy and coast guard had spent weeks on a costly and unsuccessful search for them. Now, many editors said, Amelia was carelessly risking not only her own neck, but also a repeat of that search. The sponsors of Amelia's flight, the Hawaiian sugar cane and pineapple growers, talked about backing out.

Amelia was hurt by the criticism, but she would not let it stop her. But she had to wait for several days, while the weather was too uncertain for her flight. She spent the time swimming, visiting a volcano on the island of Hawaii, and writing a "popping off" letter to George. "If I do not do a good job it will not be because the plane and motor are not excellent nor because women cannot fly."

On the morning of January 11 there was a downpour over Honolulu. That meant a dangerous amount of mud on the Wheeler Field runways, which were not paved. But if Amelia did not leave that afternoon, the weather over her route might not be good enough for several more days.

Climbing into her bright red Vega, Amelia

waited for her mechanic to pry a large ball of mud and grass off the tail skid. She noticed the three fire engines and the ambulance ready on the runway, in case the Vega's heavy load of fuel burst into flames. Then she took off from Wheeler Field in sprays of mud— but safely.

During this flight Amelia was the first civilian to have two-way radiotelephone contact with the surface. George, back in Honolulu, was greatly reassured to hear her voice from time to time instead of suffering through the long silence until she landed. For Amelia, it was a nuisance to reel the radio antenna in and out through a hole in the cockpit floor, but she was almost as happy to hear George's voice as he was to hear hers. Radio audiences, too, were thrilled when Amelia's messages were broadcast on commercial stations. "Everything okay," she told them cheerfully.

Flying west to east, night came quickly. It

was a night "of tropic loveliness," Amelia wrote later. "Stars hung outside my cockpit window close enough to touch." Later, flying through a bank of clouds with the plane window open, she became chilled. She sipped hot chocolate from her thermos, "the most interesting cup of hot chocolate I have ever had, sitting up eight thousand feet over the middle of the Pacific, quite alone."

Eighteen hours and sixteen minutes out of Honolulu, Amelia landed at the Oakland, California, airport. A crowd of over ten thousand cheered her and showered her with roses. They would have torn her plane apart for souvenirs, if the mechanics hadn't quickly shut it in a hangar. There was an enormous celebration in Oakland, including a salute from eleven navy planes. President Roosevelt sent Amelia his congratulations, and Eleanor Roosevelt urged Amelia to come visit the White House whenever she was in Washington, D.C.

* * *

Anyone else might have taken a vacation at this point, but Amelia had a heavy schedule of lectures that spring. Besides, she was already planning her next challenge: the first nonstop flight from Los Angeles to Mexico City, and the first nonstop flight from Mexico City to Newark, New Jersey. The Mexican government encouraged her plans, hoping to promote goodwill with the United States and to attract tourists to Mexico.

On the clear moonlit night of April 19, 1935, Amelia took off from the Burbank airport. This flight went smoothly, except that she had to land on a dry lakebed fifty miles short of Mexico City. Again, a huge crowd cheered her when she arrived at the Mexico City airport. The Mexican government issued a special commemorative stamp (airmail, of course) with Amelia's name and the date.

On her return, Amelia aimed to set

another record, flying nonstop over the Gulf of Mexico and on to Newark, New Jersey. Again, she had to wait for several days for favorable weather. Then the hardest part of the trip—the takeoff, because Mexico City sits at a high altitude, where the air is thin. Since Amelia's plane had to be heavily laden with fuel for the long flight, she needed an extra-long runway—three miles—to gain enough speed to become airborne. The Mexican government obligingly bulldozed a special runway for her on mudflats a few miles from Mexico City.

"Slowly I rose to 10,000 feet," Amelia wrote later, "to skim over the mountains that hem in the central valley where the city lies . . . Majestic Popocatepetl raised its snowy head to the south, luminous in the rays of the rising sun." It was such a beautiful scene that she was almost distracted "from the task at hand, that of herding a heavy plane out of that great upland saucer."

The shortest distance between Mexico City and Newark included a seven-hundred-mile stretch over the Gulf of Mexico. Amelia had flown long distances over both the Atlantic and the Pacific, but not during the daytime and with such clear weather. No clouds or fog blocked her view of the water. "The Gulf of Mexico looked large. And wet," she wrote. She was very much aware that the Vega had only one engine, and that even the best engines could "develop indigestion." This, she decided, would be her last flight over water in a single-engine plane.

As she flew on north, George urged her by radio to end the trip at Washington, D.C., but Amelia was not about to stop now. At the Newark airport she was mobbed by wildly cheering fans, who carried her to the hangar on their shoulders. She was the first person to make this nonstop flight of 2,100 miles—another new record. Reporters noticed that she didn't even look tired, after fourteen hours and eighteen minutes of straight flying.

Amelia hardly paused to rest before going on with her lecture schedule. Two months later, the hectic pace finally caught up with her. She wrote her mother from a hospital in Los Angeles. "Yes, here I am again. The sinus is kicking up . . . so Dr. Goldstein is going to work on me tomorrow."

In her next letter, while she was recovering from the sinus surgery, Amelia took a bossy tone with her mother. "Please remember you and Pidge attract attention as my relatives . . . I'd prefer you to get a few simple decent clothes, both of you." She went on with advice about where Amy should go for her summer vacation. These days, Amelia often sounded more like the mother than her mother did.

Amelia's schedule for the fall of 1935 was crammed fuller than usual, if that was possible. In September, flying out of Denver with

George and Paul Mantz, she thought about her mother's girlhood travels in Colorado and her story of being the first woman to ride up Pike's Peak. Amelia wrote her mother as they flew by the mountain, describing it as "pretty bald, kind of pinkish above the timber line. The valleys to the left are filled with fog very white in that bright sun.

"We hope to stop at Grand Canyon Airport for lunch," Amelia ended the letter. "Then on to Burbank in the afternoon." Reading this, Amy must have remembered her snail-pace journey to Colorado in 1890, and shaken her head in wonder.

Besides all her speaking engagements, Amelia spent a month that fall at Purdue University in Indiana. The president of Purdue had hired her especially to encourage young women to follow careers. At that time, schools of engineering and agriculture were as good as closed to women. Young women who studied at Purdue were expected to major in home economics, preparing themselves to get married and run households. So it was thrilling for the women students to hear Amelia say things like, "Many divorces are caused by the complete dependence of the female."

Aside from anything she said, Amelia inspired the female students just by her example. After all, *she* was successful, famous, attractive, and popular. *And* she was married to George Putnam, a handsome, successful, charming man who was proud of her independence and accomplishments.

But Amelia couldn't be content with what she had already accomplished. The next year, 1936, Amelia faced her thirty-ninth birthday in July. She was not getting any younger. Competitive flying was just as demanding as an athletic sport, because a pilot needed great stamina, alertness, and quick reflexes. Now or never was the time for Amelia to try for one last spectacular record-breaking flight.

Of course Amelia knew that other pilots had died, going for one last spectacular flight. It had just happened to two of her friends, the pilot Wiley Post and the humorist Will Rogers. Last August the two men had crashed Post's Vega in a swamp near Barrow, Alaska, on their way to an Arctic Circle flight. Amelia and George had talked and laughed with them, only a few days before, at Will Rogers's ranch.

Amelia grieved for her friends, but grief and fear of danger would not keep her from trying to break one more record. So far, no one had flown all the way around the world at its greatest circumference, the equator. Such a round-the-world trip would need even more preparation than any of Amelia's other adventures.

For one thing, Amelia would need a new plane, and she already had her eye on the double-engine Lockheed 10E Electra. Purdue University agreed to buy the plane for her through the Purdue Research Foundation. The idea was that Amelia would use the flight to test the strains of long-distance flying on the crew and equipment.

The route also had to be carefully planned. Some countries on the equator, such as Muscat on the Arabian Peninsula, did not allow planes to fly over their territory. Others, such as Brazil, had great stretches of jungle, where a forced landing would be very dangerous. At every planned stop, fuel and equipment for repairs must be waiting.

George Putnam used all his connections to get Amelia's new adventure off the ground. A friend and author at Standard Oil arranged the fuel stations. Another friend, Gene Vidal, now director of the Bureau of Air Commerce in Washington, got the U.S. Navy to contribute information on weather over the Pacific. The U.S. State Department had to get permission from every country that Amelia would fly over or land in.

The flight over the vast Pacific Ocean would be the greatest challenge. At first Amelia thought she would have to refuel in the air between Tokyo and Hawaii, and she persuaded the navy to help her refuel over their base on Midway Island. But in-flight refueling would be tricky—for one thing, there was the danger of catching the refueling hose in the propeller of the Electra. Besides, the length of that leg—twenty-four hours without rest or relief—would be grueling for Amelia.

Then George learned about Howland Island, a tiny dot between New Guinea and Hawaii. The U.S. Navy was planning to build an emergency landing field there. If Amelia could use that field, she could refuel there in the usual way, on land. That seemed like a much better solution, and so the route was changed.

For technical assistance, Amelia hired Paul

Mantz again. In June 1936 they flew to Los Angeles to look at the Lockheed plane she had ordered. On Amelia's birthday, July 24, she officially took possession of this powerful state-of-the-art plane.

The Electra was over thirty-eight feet long, with a wingspan of fifty-five feet. With its two engines of 550 horsepower each, it could cruise faster than two hundred miles per hour. Its cabin was fully pressurized, which meant the pilot could fly at high altitudes without suffering from lack of oxygen. Under ideal conditions, it could fly as far as four thousand miles without refueling.

"I could write poetry about this ship," exclaimed Amelia after flying her Electra to Kansas City. At this point, no one was thinking of the fact that Electra, in Greek mythology, was the *lost* star of the Pleiades.

By this time Amelia and George had bought a house in North Hollywood, and there they did a great deal of the planning for her round-the-world trip. She would take scientific equipment to gather samples and take measurements during the flight. She would take emergency supplies, including rubber rafts and machetes.

Amelia had equipment installed to make her plane safer: an automatic pilot, a radio that could operate on both the standard aviation frequencies and the emergency frequency, and a radio direction finder. The direction finder guided the pilot to his destination by fixing on a radio signal from that place.

Although Amelia would be the only pilot, she would need to take a navigator with her, especially for the tricky route over the Pacific Ocean. She decided on Harry Manning, a ship's captain, whom she had first met in 1928 on her way back from Europe.

In February 1937, after planning the trip for several months, Amelia held a press conference to announce her attempt to fly around the world. Her plan was to fly east across the Pacific Ocean, from Oakland to Honolulu to Howland Island to Lae, New Guinea, and on around the world. On the afternoon of March 17, the Electra took off from the Oakland field with Amelia, Paul Mantz, Harry Manning, and a second navigator, Fred Noonan, on board.

Paul would make final arrangements for the next stages of the journey, then stay behind in Hawaii. Fred would be her principal navigator as far as Howland Island, since he knew the Pacific Ocean so well. While Fred was on board, Harry would concentrate on working the radio, mainly the 500-kilocycle frequency. That was the band used by ships at sea and most coastal stations, so it could give them valuable information about their position and the weather ahead. It would also be the most helpful in case of an emergency.

The Electra reached Hawaii in record time, in spite of problems with one of the propellers and the generator for the radio. But by the time the plane approached the Honolulu airport, there was serious tension between Paul Mantz and Amelia. With Paul at the controls, the plane made a rough landing.

We Pay with Courage

In Hawaii, Amelia only had to wait two days for good flight weather. The whole world was waiting with her. The *Herald Tribune*, which had bought exclusive rights to her story, was eager for the next installment.

The U.S. Coast Guard cutter *Itasca* was standing by off Howland Island, to guide Amelia's plane in. A technician had already started for Karachi, India, to be on hand to overhaul the Electra's engines when Amelia eventually landed there. Ten thousand special envelopes were on board the Electra, to be carried around the world, postmarked, autographed by Amelia, and sold to collectors at five dollars an envelope.

At dawn on March 20, with Harry Manning and Fred Noonan aboard, Amelia taxied down the concrete runway of the navy's Luke Field, near Pearl Harbor. But the runway was slick from rain, and the plane, heavily loaded with fuel, veered from side to side. Then the landing gear on the right collapsed, sending the plane into a ground loop and a crash in a shower of sparks. Gasoline poured into the belly of the plane. Luckily Amelia had already turned off the engines, so there was no fire.

No one was hurt. But the plane's landing gear was stripped off, and one wing was crumpled. Amelia climbed out of the cabin door and onto the runway to see her beautiful Electra lying on its belly. She felt a stab of pain, as if she had been hurt, for her "battered bird with broken wings."

Amelia was shaken and deeply disappointed. All the months of hard work, all the money, all the careful preparation—wrecked, along with her plane. But even in the instant before the crash, her thought had been, *If we don't burn up, I want to try again.*

She knew George would feel the same way. And although he was badly shaken, too, he sent her an encouraging telegram from California. "Whether you want to call it a day or keep going later," George told Amelia, "is equally jake with me."

Some people in aviation blamed Amelia for the accident. One writer called her round-the-world flight a "racket" undertaken merely for "quick fortune and fame." Amelia was hurt, but she kept her feelings to herself. Privately, she thought the landing gear had collapsed because it had been weakened by Paul Mantz's rough landing at Honolulu.

Shipping the Electra back to Los Angeles and having it repaired at the Lockheed airport would delay the trip for another two months and cost an extra $25,000. All the other changes in Amelia's plans would cost another $25,000. George and Amelia had to ask friends to contribute the money, an enormous amount for those days.

Because of the delay, Amelia decided to change her route and fly west to east. The monsoon season in the Caribbean and Africa was approaching, and if she flew over those areas first, she would miss the worst of the bad weather. Also, she would be flying with the prevailing winds, which would cut down on her flying time and fuel use. The main drawback was that now the flight to tiny Howland Island would come near the end of the journey. This was the most difficult stretch of the route, and Amelia and Fred would be tired by that time.

May 21, 1937, was five years and one day after the start of Amelia's solo flight across the Atlantic. Without any announcement, she took off from the Oakland airfield, headed east. In Miami she would pause for a few days to have her plane thoroughly checked over, then make her final decision about whether to try the round-the-world flight.

There were still minor problems with the Electra, and Amelia was still thinking about which equipment was absolutely necessary and which only added weight. In California she had decided to leave behind the emergency-frequency radio, operating at 500 kilocycles, which Harry Manning had favored. The Electra's other radio, using the 6210 and 3105 bandwidths, did not work well in tests in Miami. The technicians believed the aerials were part of the problem, and Amelia finally decided to take off the 250-foot trailing aerial. It added to the weight of the plane, and it was a nuisance to reel it out and in.

On the second start around the world, Fred Noonan was with Amelia, but not Harry

Manning. Harry had dropped off of Amelia's crew to return to his ship, and Fred Noonan would navigate the entire distance. Fred was one of the best navigators in the business, with years of experience in Latin America and the Pacific. At Pan American he'd had a problem with heavy drinking, but he swore he was reformed now.

Now that Amelia was confident about attempting her round-the-world trip again, she and George welcomed reporters and photographers. At their Miami hotel, in front of newsreel cameras, they put on a kind of comedy routine. "Now, are you sure you don't want me to come along?" George asked his wife with a smile.

"Well, of course you know I think a lot of you," Amelia teased him, "but one hundred and eighty pounds of gasoline . . . perhaps might be a little more valuable."

George pretended to be shocked and hurt. "You mean you prefer one hundred and eighty pounds of gasoline to one hundred and eighty pounds of husband?"

Amelia giggled. "I think you've guessed right."

From Miami, Amelia wrote her mother a quick last note: "Hope to take off tomorrow A.M. to San Juan, Puerto Rico. Here is three hundred bucks." As usual, she signed herself "A."

Before dawn on June 1, Amelia and Fred drove to the Miami airport with everything they would need for the flight. They had pith helmets and machetes, in case they were forced down in the jungle. Amelia's thermoses were full of hot tomato juice, while Fred's held coffee. Amelia's suitcase was packed with a few shirts and slacks and underwear, one pair of shoes, and a coverall for mechanical work.

The summer morning was still cool as Amelia and George spent a moment alone in the hangar, while the mechanic worked on the Electra. At about 6:00 A.M., Amelia climbed into the cockpit and sat down in front of the control panel. George climbed up on the wing to shake hands with Fred and kiss his wife good-bye one more time. She closed the hatch of the cockpit, and the roar of the engines rose. Then the silver Electra, with the black, orange, and red stripes on its wings, rushed down the runway, lifted easily, and disappeared into the rising sun.

The flight from Miami to Puerto Rico went smoothly, and so did the flights to Venezuela and Brazil. Amelia in her cockpit, and Fred, in the cabin behind her at the navigator's table, gazed down on the Caribbean Sea, then on rivers winding through dense jungle. In one of the articles she cabled home, Amelia joked that with an autopilot and a world-class navigator on board, "long-range flying was becoming pretty sissy."

From Natal, Brazil, Amelia and Fred flew on across the South Atlantic Ocean. They were heading for Dakar, Senegal, on the west coast of Africa. But as they approached land, the coast was hidden in mist, and they couldn't see any landmarks. At this point Amelia seemed to lose confidence in her navigator. Fred advised her to head south, but she thought they were already south of Dakar. She turned north instead, and had to land in St. Louis, Senegal.

Flying on over Africa, Amelia remembered her fantasy adventures long ago, when she was a girl in Kansas. Then, it had been thrilling just to say the names of the exotic places: Timbuktu, El Fasher, Khartoum. She had imagined traveling to them on camels or elephants. Now she was *flying* over them. Even daring, imaginative Millie had never thought of an adventure so wild.

In Karachi, India (now in Pakistan), Amelia and Fred took time to ride camels. They were over halfway around the world, on schedule. Fred wrote his wife that Amelia was "a grand person for such a trip. . . . In addition to being a fine companion she can take hardship as well as a man, and work like one."

Amelia called George on the telephone, enthusiastic. She felt "swell." Everything about the trip was going so well. "We'll do it again, together, sometime," she promised him.

From Karachi, Amelia flew the 1,390 miles to Calcutta. This flight went smoothly, too, except for a flock of black eagles that surrounded the plane at one point. Landing at Calcutta, Amelia called George again. But this time she told him, "I'm starting to have personnel trouble."

George thought she meant that Fred Noonan was drinking again. "Stop the flight right there and don't take any chances," he urged. But Amelia thought she could "handle the situation." She agreed to call again after she reached New Guinea.

In Calcutta, bad weather hit. Through torrents of rain, Amelia and Fred made their way slowly to Akyab and Rangoon, Burma; to Singapore; and to Bandung in Java (now Indonesia). They had to stay in Bandung for a whole week while the Dutch mechanics adjusted some of the instruments.

To fill in the time, Amelia and Fred went sightseeing and shopping, and again Amelia talked to George, back in New York. She told him she expected to be back in California before the Fourth of July, in time for the big Independence Day celebration he was planning. "Good night, hon," said Amelia at the end of their conversation. "Good night," George answered. "I'll be sitting in Oakland waiting for you."

After a stop on Timor Island, Amelia reached Port Darwin, Australia, on Monday, June 28. Here the direction finder receiver on Amelia's radio was repaired, and she left the parachutes behind to save weight. "A parachute would not help over the Pacific," she said cheerfully.

The next day they took off for Lae, New Guinea. Amelia had been traveling for over a month since she left California. Most of that time she had spent in the Electra's cockpit— four feet eight inches high by four feet six inches wide by four feet six inches deep— with little sleep or food. Maybe at this point she was thinking, Only three more stops: Howland Island, Honolulu—and home.

In Lae, more work was done on the Electra's radio. Amelia telegraphed George: "RADIO MISUNDERSTANDING AND PERSONNEL UNFITNESS PROBABLY WILL HOLD ONE DAY . . ." By "radio misunderstanding," she most likely meant she had discovered something disturbing about the *Itasca*, the coast guard cutter that was to help guide Amelia to Howland Island. The *Itasca* didn't have the radio equipment to take bearings on the Electra on the 1305 bandwidth. "Personnel unfitness" possibly meant that Fred Noonan had been drinking heavily.

The weather forecast on the morning of July 2 predicted headwinds and local squalls over Amelia's course from New Guinea to Howland Island, but generally good visibility and no major storms. At 10 A.M. the Electra, weighted down with one thousand gallons of fuel, roared down the unpaved runway. It barely cleared the drop-off at the end of the runway and sank to within a few feet of the ocean before leveling off. Other pilots, watching the takeoff, praised Amelia's handling of the plane with such an overload.

From the beginning, Amelia had known that the flight to Howland would be the biggest challenge. As she had remarked in 1934, before her first flight to Hawaii, "It's easier to hit a continent than an island." Now she was trying to hit a very small island in a poorly charted ocean. Fred Noonan would need all his navigational skills, and all the help he could get from ships and the ground. He had to keep the Electra on course for the

2,556 miles from Lae to Howland, or they would miss the two-mile-long dot of an island.

The U. S. Navy and Coast Guard were doing their best to help Amelia Earhart to a safe landing on Howland Island. They had marked the new runways with red flags and shooed thousands of frigate birds and terns off them. The coast guard cutter *Itasca* waited off Howland Island, in case of emergency.

Between Lae and Howland the USS *Ontario* stood by, to help guide Amelia by radio. Unfortunately the *Ontario* was an outdated ship, with old-fashioned radio equipment. During that night the *Ontario* regularly broadcast a signal by Morse code, as Amelia had requested, but the ship never heard any acknowledgment from the Electra.

Seven hours and twenty minutes out of Lae, Amelia reported her position by radio.

The Electra was about twenty miles southwest of the Nukumanu Islands, on course for Howland. Amelia had thought that her one thousand gallons of fuel would be ample for the long flight—eighteen hours, she estimated. But the headwinds during the first part of the trip were much stronger than forecast. By this time she knew that the flight would take well over twenty hours, instead.

Twenty hours was dangerously close to the Electra's fuel margin. Amelia was now a third of the way into the flight—time to return to New Guinea, if going on was too risky. She flew on, into the night. If the Electra stayed on course, they would arrive at Howland Island about two hours after sunrise.

As dawn broke in the clear skies over Howland, the coast guard cutter *Itasca*, stationed near the island, sent up a column of black smoke to help guide Amelia in. The plan had been for Amelia to radio the *Itasca* every half hour for weather reports and to check her position. As agreed, the *Itasca* broadcast weather reports every hour and half hour.

But the Electra's radio equipment must not have been working properly. Fourteen hours and fifteen minutes after the Electra took off from Lae, the *Itasca* began to hear Amelia's voice. She was asking them to broadcast position fixes at 3105 frequency. That was exactly what the coast guard was already doing. Amelia wasn't receiving any of the coast guard's reports, although several other stations in the Pacific, it turned out later, had overheard them clearly.

Amelia's first message was hard to understand, but they heard her say something about "cloudy weather." An hour later, in a clearer message, she said the weather was "overcast." Then Amelia's messages began coming more often, and more urgently, asking for bearings.

An hour and fifteen minutes after sunrise at Howland Island, the *Itasca* heard Amelia

again: "We must be on you but cannot see you but gas is running low have been unable reach you by radio we are flying at 1000 feet." If the Electra had been anywhere near Howland, Amelia could have seen the island out her cockpit window, because the weather was clear there.

But to the northwest, the skies were overcast. Amelia and Fred must have been off course in that direction, and unable to receive the radio messages that could have corrected their course. Half an hour later, Amelia radioed that they had finally received signals from the *Itasca*, but the signals came in too faintly to help.

At twenty hours and fourteen minutes after Amelia's takeoff from Lae, she sent another radio message, repeating what she and Fred thought their position was. They thought they had flown far enough east, estimating the distance by the time and their speed. "We are now running north and

south," she said. They were spending the last of their fuel flying back and forth over where they thought Howland Island must be.

The *Itasca* radioed the emergency to coast guard headquarters in San Francisco, where George had been waiting since Amelia took off from Lae. Then the coast guard cutter steamed away from Howland to search the overcast ocean to the northwest, where they judged Amelia must have come down. When they reached that area, the sea was rough, with waves six feet high.

The *Itasca* kept on broadcasting as they searched, but there were no more messages from the Electra. Meanwhile, a navy seaplane started out from Honolulu to join the search, but it was forced to turn back by bad weather.

George called Amy Earhart, waiting at the house in North Hollywood, and told her the bad news.

A complete search, with an aircraft carrier

and its sixty-two planes, was launched several days later. The searchers covered 150,000 square miles of ocean and islands—and turned up nothing.

Since the last word was heard from Amelia Earhart in July 1937, many people have spent years trying to figure out exactly what happened to her. Dozens of books and hundreds of articles have been written about her. She was such a beloved heroine that people longed for a conclusion to the mystery of her disappearance. Some writers suggested that Amelia and Fred managed to climb into their life raft and paddle to an island, where they were somehow overlooked by the search. One journalist even claimed that Amelia and Fred were actually on a secret mission for the U.S. government, and that the Japanese had captured, questioned, and executed them.

But the probable answer seems to be the sad, simple one that Muriel Earhart

Morrissey believed. She knew that her sister would have had to make a dead-stick landing on rough seas, possibly knocking her unconscious. And some other Lockheed Electras, when forced to land on water, had sunk quickly. "It seems to me most likely," wrote Muriel in *Amelia, My Courageous Sister* ". . . that Amelia's plane was submerged within minutes after her last radio message and probably within one hundred miles of Howland Island."

We may never know for sure what happened to Amelia Earhart. But how her life changed the world is well known.

With her record-breaking flights, she demonstrated what women could do in aviation. Her achievements also encouraged more passengers to use air travel, and stimulated airplane designers and manufacturers to build faster, safer, more comfortable airplanes.

She helped organize women fliers, the Ninety-Nines. This association of women pilots now has over 6,500 members and gives yearly Amelia Earhart awards for flight training. Zonta, the organization of business and professional women to which Amelia belonged, gives Amelia Earhart Fellowships to women for aerospace-connected science and engineering.

She announced over and over, calmly and confidently, that women deserve the same opportunities as men. And her actions backed up her words.

Before her solo flight across the Atlantic in 1932, Amelia had written George a letter to be read in case she died in the attempt. "Women must try to do things as men have tried. When they fail, their failure must be but a challenge to others." Amelia Earhart's life is still an inspiration to girls and women who dream of launching adventures, going after careers, breaking out of limits. Her example urges them to follow their dreams with energy, patience—and high courage.